Two hearts collide ...

Zoey Appleton, who's idyllic young life is shattered by the most senseless of tragedies, but whose passionate heart never dies. **Tristan March,** raised in the wilds of Alaska and the paradise of Hawaii, a thrill-seeker who finds beauty in every woman, but has never, ever believed in true love.

... at University Hospital

University

HOSPITAL

CHERIE BENNETT
and
JEFF GOTTESFELD

BERKLEY JAM BOOKS, NEW YORK

This is a work of fiction. Names, characters, places, and incidents are either the products of the author's imagination or are used fictitiously, and any resemblance to actual persons, living or dead, business establishments, events or locales is entirely coincidental.

UNIVERSITY HOSPITAL

A Berkley Jam Book / published by arrangement with
the author

PRINTING HISTORY
Berkley Jam edition / October 1999

The Penguin Putnam Inc. World Wide Web site address is
http://www.penguinputnam.com

ISBN: 0-425-17144-2

BERKLEY JAM BOOKS®
Berkley Jam Books are published by The Berkley Publishing Group,
a division of Penguin Putnam Inc.,
375 Hudson Street, New York, New York 10014.
BERKLEY JAM and its logo are trademarks belonging to
Penguin Putnam Inc.

PRINTED IN THE UNITED STATES OF AMERICA

10 9 8 7 6 5 4 3 2 1

For our families

University
HOSPITAL

prologue

ZOEY

Okay, so Erin was coming over. Our plan was:

a) rent videos

b) drool over hunk *du jour*

c) plan next day's imminent escape from the burbs, hallelujah, can I get an amen, please?

Doorbell rings, I scuff through the palatial hallway of my brother and sister-in-law's overdone mini-mansion—I live there but it is definitely *not* home—to let in number-one girlfriend.

And there she is.

Now get this: I am clad, per usual, in some variation on the jeans, T-shirt thing. And here is Erin: postage-stamp mini. Very-cropped crop top. Slut puppy heels. Makeup to the max. All in pink.

This is *so* not Erin.

Both of us fall somewhere between we-don't-shave-on-principle-Paula-Cole-wannabes and cashmere-clad-French-manicured-Gwyneth-wannabes. I am taller, more athletic, much more studious. As in, class salutatorian who would not be caught dead on a date with valedictorian if you paid me. Erin is blonder, lazier, and tends to the dramatic.

When we used to watch *Dawson's* back in tenth grade we joked that I was Joey and she was Jen, but we both lacked a Dawson. Alas, true then, true now.

Also true: Erin is the only real friend I made during my three-year tenure—read: *prison sentence*—in the soul-numbing hell that is Belle Woods, Oklahoma.

Basically, Erin saved my life.

So I let her in. She strikes a pose, thrusting out both chest and lower lip.

"If you're going for a Neo-Nymphette Trailer Trash kinda look, you succeeded," say I. "Did the costume party slip my mind?"

"Nope." She grins hugely through spackled pink lip gloss. "Grab your whatever, we're outta here."

"I thought we were renting videos."

"Were. Past tense. I'll tell you in the car 'cuz if Karen sees me she'll give bir— Oh, hi, Karen. How's life?"

My sister-in-law Karen, a.k.a. Skank Socialite From Hell, a.k.a. Possessed She-Devil Whom My

Brother Married In A Moment Of Mental Imbalance That Appears To Be Ongoing, marches into hallway. Takes in Erin.

Every inch of Karen's bony for-God's-sake-eat-a-hamburger! designer-clad frame quivers in indignation.

I *love* that part.

Typical Karen remark to Erin: "You actually walked out of your house looking like that?"

Typical me comeback to Karen: "No, she borrowed your broom and flew on it, you anorexic witch." Alas, too many of my best comebacks remain internal. Read: per usual, I didn't say it out loud.

"You know, I believe I did," Erin actually replies, all earnest solemnity. Then she grabs my arm and drags me toward the door. "Lovely chatting with you, Karen. Love the new ensemble. Ralph Lauren, isn't it? Nautical is so *you*."

"Just a moment, ladies." Karen folds her *faux* sailor shirt-clad arms. "Where are you going, Zoey?"

"I have no idea, actually."

"I'm kidnapping her," says nearly nude Erin. "Kiss-kiss, Karen, don't wait up!"

"Zoey, come back thi—"

Too late, we're gone.

Whooping with laughter, we jump into Erin's trashed-out Miata. She peals out of the circular driveway, cranks up Lucinda Williams, and screams with delight. "Did you see the look on her face? Like we got crocked and urped on her Farregamos! Well, like

I did. The oldest living virgin in Belle Woods, namely you, doesn't drink. Ergo urping while crocked is not a Zoey possibility. Do you have any idea how obnoxious you are, by the by?''

''Only because you tell me so often.''

''Hey, what are best friends for?'' She turns onto the freeway and sings along with the music, and that carries us for ten minutes.

We get off onto the freeway service road.

''Where *are* we going? My plane leaves at, like, eight in the morning.''

''And I leave tomorrow night on my backpack-youth-hostel bootie call across Europe—don't worry, safe sex is my middle name.''

''Yeah, but—''

''And in the fall we both start college. Which makes this our last night in Belle Woods, which struck me as something to celebrate in some wild, insane, one-night-only fashion. Learn how to drive!'' she yells as she zooms around someone going the actual speed limit.

''Such as?''

But Erin isn't talking. She just cranks the music louder, drives like a woman with a death wish, and finally pulls into the crowded parking lot of someplace the neon sign informs us is called CAFE AU LAID.

CAFE AU LAID is a brick building complete with red carpet and steroid-enhanced door guy in a tux, minus a shirt.

Were it not for the discreet neon sign under the

jumbo neon sign, you wouldn't know it was a strip club.

"You're kidding," I say.

Erin turns to me, eyes flashing. "It's amateur night. First the R-rated contest, meaning you strip down to the teeniest bikini you can find. Later on is skin-to-win. Use your imagination."

"And we're here because—?"

"What did I look like when you moved to Belle Woods three years ago?"

I shrug. "You, three years younger."

"Me, three years *fatter*. Delia Lamont used to moo at me when I walked down the hall."

"Delia Lamont is ambulatory E-coli with breasts."

"Whatever, everyone still laughed. Then I lost weight. When I was fat, I always had this fantasy to get really cute and strip. Now I'm really cute."

"Have you shared this with the people at *Springer*? I hear they pay airfare."

"Seriously. I did get cute, didn't I?"

"Seriously. The cutest."

Erin leans toward me. "I was looking through CDs at the mall this afternoon and I overheard the one and only Delia say she was entering the amateur contest tonight. Well, guess what? One of us is going to kick her butt."

Before I can correct her seriously misguided notion that I might actually publicly shed to music, Erin's out of the car, heading for Studboy at the door. Given few options, I trot after her.

"Watchin' or strippin'?" Studboy asks, beyond bored.

"Strippin'," Erin replies.

"Watching," I say at the same time.

"No cover for you, ten big ones for you." Studboy holds out a meaty palm. "Plus I need to see picture ID."

We haul out our proof, Erin signs up, tells him what music she wants, and pays my cover. She asks Studboy if she gets her money back if I get on stage, and Studboy says only in skin-to-win.

We sashay inside.

It's very dark, no shocker there. Looks like a disco, retro chic, complete with gag-me Boy George soundtrack. Girls are dancing everywhere—on the stage in the center, on small platforms scattered around, in cages suspended from the ceiling.

They wear bikinis so skimpy you'd think they were pitching full body wax.

The young and oh-so-hip of both sexes sit at small high-tops, dance near the stage, ogle, or all of the above. Thank God, no middle-aged guys with raincoats on their laps.

But still.

"Not even," comes from my mouth. I am grossed out.

Undeterred, Erin leads the way to one of the few empty tables. We get checked out big time. Erin checks back. Serious eye contact. By the time we reach our high-top, so does early-twenties Buzz Cut with great shoulders and multiple earrings. He and Erin head to the dance floor.

I turn down Cowboy Hat In Need Of A Good Dermatologist and sit, slightly removed—read: superior to—it all.

I'm no longer in a hip strip club somewhere near Belle Woods, somewhere near Oklahoma City.

I'm back in Chaney.

I'm home.

Chaney, Oklahoma. Pop: 8,423. You've never heard of it. Very picture-postcard pretty. Farms. Landmark houses. Families that go back generations. Including mine.

A memory: me, little, curled up on the chintz-covered window seat in my bedroom, watching dust particles dance in the sunbeams. I'm convinced they are atoms only I can see. Clearly I have superpowers. I share this secret with my father. He listens; doesn't laugh or correct me. It is only years later that I understand the banal truth of dust.

I can still see my father, listening.

Everyone knows my parents. Loves them. Me, most of all. Unlike my older brother, Kevin, lawyer groom of the Skank Socialite From Hell. He went to OU law school and a big-firm job in OKC.

Me, I never want to leave. What I want is my parents' life. My plan: college, med school, then home to Chaney. Doctor and Doctor and *Doctor* Appleton on the shingle.

Mom's fiftieth birthday, Dad pulls out two tickets to Paris. Just him and his bride, he says. They kiss me good-bye at breakfast, go to OKC to get passports, so happy.

During algebra the principal comes over the loudspeaker and says the Murrah Building in downtown OKC has been bombed. TVs go on and everyone says: how terrible. I think: my parents are near there, they can help.

Dad dies instantly. Mom lives. Trapped under the rubble, for hours. Calling for my father. For me. Until finally she stops calling when she bleeds to death.

That's what they tell me, only in a nice way so I won't get upset. And I don't. Never. Not even when I have to leave Chaney and all my friends and my real life and move to OKC suburb of Belle Woods to live with my brother and the Skank Socialite From Hell.

With the exception of Erin, I make no friends, keep my nose to the academic grindstone and my eye on the prize: go to med school, be a doctor, go back to Chaney, get my life back.

It's only at night that the monsters come.

My mother, buried alive, calling for me, only I can't move, can't breathe, gasping for air but there is no air and—

"Are we havin' fun yet?"

Erin's voice. I blink, snap back to CAFE AU LAID. She's sipping a soda, Buzz Cut and Dermatologically Challenged Cowboy by her side.

"So, you strippin'?" DC Cowboy asks me. His southern accent weighs more than he does.

"Not me. Her."

DC Cowboy grins. "Aw, I bet you're hidin' one hot bod under that T-shirt, girl."

"Gee, now you've convinced me," I reply.

"You hafta understand about my frien' Zoey," Erin slurs slightly; I realize there's more than Coke in her Coke, and it's not the first, either. "She's, like, this genius, okay? Tomorrow she's flyin' off to—where?"

"Fable Harbor, Massachusetts."

"Yeah. She's spendin' the summer at this big ol' hospital with a bunch of other teen geniuses who get to be geniuses together. See, she's gonna be a doctor."

"Don't you hafta go to medical school for that?" Buzz Cut asks.

Clearly, Erin has not hooked up with the future winners of a Nobel Prize.

"It's a summer program before freshman year of college," I explain. "Called SCRUBS. Med school comes a lot later."

Suddenly Erin grabs my arm. "Look! Over there. Delia and the Poison Perfect People! I *tol'* you! Yo, Delia!"

Erin screams and starts to lift what little shirt she's wearing to flash the Belle Woods High ultimates, but I yank it back down.

For one thing, Delia and the Triple Ps aren't looking.

For another thing, Buzz and DC Cowboy definitely are.

The MC—another shirtless, tuxedoed Studboy

type, announces R-rated amateur hour. The crowd applauds, whistles, hungry for bikini-clad meat. He calls a name, a brunette in whigger regalia runs up on stage and dances under the roving pinspots to Doctor Dre. She gets down, dirty, points toy Glocks at the guys in the audience, then licks the guns.

It's revolting.

Girl after girl is called up to perform. The audience gets rowdier, the strippers, raunchier. Thankfully, Buzz Cut and DC Cowboy move closer to the stage for an up-front and personal talent assessment.

"I had no idea so many girls share your fantasy of debasing themselves to music," I tell Erin.

She's sobering, busy assessing the frizzy-haired comp currently gyrating on stage. "Serious cellulite. This babe has not met the concept of the three-way mirror, 'cuz no way has she ever checked out that back view."

Nasty crack, the kind she usually saved only for the Skank Socialite from Hell. Not your usual Erin. "What happened to my sensitive, deep friend?" I ask.

"My bitchy alter ego is having a one-night stand," she says, flipping her hair in a bitchy fashion. Which I really hate.

So I say, "And your alter-ego is a mean, incredibly superficial exhibitionist?"

Zing. Hurt flits across her face and I hate myself. In three years Erin has never said one mean thing to me.

"You're goin' to Kenyon, Zoey," she says. "I'm goin' to OSU, and we both know I barely got in. You have your whole future planned out. Me? I'm clueless and scared to death. There's only two things I'm sure of. I want to get the hell out of Belle Woods. And just once I want to say I was cuter than Delia Lamont."

I'm about to do penance by going into supportive-friend mode when the MC shouts out Delia's name. High School Bitch Goddess (Named by Acclaim) runs up on stage to the thunderous applause and whistles of her buds.

Delia wears a long, slinky black gown slit to heaven. Gives "retro" new meaning by slipping it off to "Hey, Big Spender." It's a pre-dye-job Marilyn Monroe kinda moment.

The crowd goes berserk. DC Cowboy is so psyched he's yelling, "I swahr she's buck-nekked under thar!" over Eydie Gourmet.

Delia isn't, of course. Said gown falls to reveal high-cut black teddie, which gives way to black thong bikini the approximate size of three Cindy Crawford beauty marks. DC Cowboy apparently passes out from excitement.

My eyes slide over to Erin. Jaw set hard. Eyes that could freeze flint.

And all she says is, "I can take her."

Delia finishes to the big O. As in *ovation.* DC Cowboy rouses himself and lights a post-big O cigarette.

As luck would have it—read: really bad—Erin follows the Delia show. I yell good luck, but she's already running toward the stage. Lauryn Hill's hip-hop groove pounds, and suddenly it's Electric Erin. Either she's been practicing for this moment or she has natural talent. The crowd gets into it, which revs her.

Objectively, she's prettier than Delia. But Delia has three things going for her, the first two being her right and left breasts. Both are perfection. Delia Cooper's ligaments are astonishing for a girl whose 34C status is silicone-free.

Cooper's ligaments hold breast tissue in place. Or not. In which case they are called Cooper's droopers.

I am a font of useless medical information. That's why they picked me for SCRUBS.

The third thing: Delia has the High School Bitch Goddess (Named By Acclaim) invisible sheen. Always confident. Deemed more beautiful than she actually is. Capable of flattening mere mortals with a single syllable.

In this case, the syllable is: "Moo."

The music pounds and Erin grooves under the lights, triumphant in a pink bikini.

Delia's voice cuts through it all. "Moo!"

Then louder. *"Moo!"* Her entourage joins in.

"Moo-oo!", *"MOO-OO!"* through cupped hands, over and over.

Meaningless to the crowd, it decimates Erin, the obvious point. She falters, reduced to old chubby tenth-grade self. I'm ready to put my fist through Delia's face.

I don't.

Erin rallies momentarily, getting down with her bad self. Then she's beyond down, over the line, trying too hard. Pathetic. Delia and friends add other barnyard noises. The crowd smells Erin's desperation. They turn on her, lead her to the *abbatoir*, ready for slaughter.

Lauryn quits singing, and Erin skulks offstage to indifferent applause and a cow choir. The MC says the winner will be announced at midnight. I lie and tell Erin she was way hotter than Delia. Buzz Cut and DC Cowboy join in the hallelujah chorus. I'm embarrassed when she believes us.

There's a commotion as some screaming girl pushes her way through the crowd. Must be drunk, no biggie. Suddenly the girl's front of us, red-faced, wild, cursing out DC Cowboy. *DC Cowboy?* She's the wife or the girlfriend, not clear which. He curses her back. They turn the volume to eleven, it gets uglier, would be funny if it wasn't so sad.

Erin whispers to me it's time to go spill drinks on Delia. I agree. We are laughing, sneaking away from the domestic blitz when I hear a loud "pop."

Fireworks?

Can't be. I turn around to ask Erin if she heard it, but weirdly she falls to the floor.

A pool of blood surrounds her head, growing larger and larger. Her eyes are open.

She looks surprised.

"I meant to shoot *him*!" DC Cowboy's girlfriend screams, aiming the gun anew at DC Cowboy. "And now I'm gonna!"

There's another shot, and the bouncer grabs her from behind and wrestles her to the floor, and people scream.

Erin's chest is rising and falling, rising and falling. She's alive. Just like in the movies, they're yelling for a doctor. *"Is there a doctor?"*

My mind says: pressure on wound. Hold hands on wound. Do not move victim. Cover victim, as body temperature will drop from shock. If victim's breathing stops, give mouth-to-mouth. Start CPR if necessary. Continue until paramedics arrive.

I know just what to do.

But my body will not move.

"Zoey?" Erin gasps.

But it isn't Erin. It's my mother, buried under ten tons of rubble that used to be the Murrah Federal Building. She is bleeding to death, calling to me to save her. But I shrink under a table, can't move, can't breathe. Can't.

When I moved to Belle Woods, Erin saved my life. And now I can't save hers.

1
ZOEY

Dear Erin-the-Body,

Okay, so here I am at Fable Harbor University Hospital (FHUH the signs say, but I dubbed it Effing-Huh! Read: I can't effing-huh! believe I'm really here). I'm in my suite in the med school dorm, and don't think "sweet," 'cuz it's just a butt-ugly room with a butt-ugly bathroom that I'll be sharing with two butt-ugly strangers. How's that for positive thinking? But I figure, hey, it's a) the start of my med ed; and b) far from The Skank; so it c) works for me.

I'm in longhand 'cuz I haven't set up my 'puter yet, but that's just the kind of best friend I am, kiss-kiss. Saw some of quaint Fable Harbor on my quaint trol-

ley here—quaint shops with quaint shoppers shopping, quaint marina with quaint boats boating, quaint ocean with quaint waves waving.

Lemme say it again, Okie Sister. OCEAN! Which I will embrace when I finish this missive, O Wounded One. Erin, did that really happen? Headline, Belle Woods Gazette: BURB BABE BATTLES BACK FROM SHOCKING SHOOTING AT STEAMY STRIP CLUB. *Now, that's grabbing the spotlight from Delia. You'd think a Medhead such as* moi *would know a shoulder wound from a head wound. I didn't. I thought you were in bad shape. Real. I was so scared.*

I know you said you were fine and you'd kick my butt if I didn't get on the plane, but I still feel major guilt that I left you. Just remember that Anal Ree's middle name is LawSuit, so go for it. This flies to your mom's best friend's daughter's flat in London, stop one on the bootie call. Listen up, you wanton hussy. As you wend across Europe leaving a trail of broken hearts, make sure there is also a trail of broken jonnie wrappers. Read: no love without the glove and all that. And the other thing is that I love you, Okie Sister. Call, write, or scream really loud in a moment of bliss, and I'll come running or applaud. Have the best summer ever.

LYMI,
Zoey-the-Mind

I reread my letter, slip it in an envelope. I still see Erin lying in a pool of blood. Flesh wound, thank God, worth a free night in the hospital and a headline in the *Gazette*.

Erin seems unaware that I froze, failed, flipped out, flucked-up. But I know. God. Thinking about it makes me feel sick. I want to be a doctor just short of how much I want to keep breathing. Tending to the wounded in a crisis is kinda helpful when pursuing a medical career.

Schlitz.

As in beer. As in I'm trying to cure myself of cursing by making up near-curses. Kinda like near-beer. Less filling but better than nothing.

I hoist my suitcase onto the bare mattress by the window and get out my running shoes. Running shuts down my mind for a while.

We're having weather, as the Skank always says. Wind's whipping, sky dark with storm clouds. Yet I'm going running by the ocean. The *ocean*! It's so *not* Oklahoma.

I smell it before I can see it—salty, fishy, alive. I round a corner, and there it is. Vast. Angry-looking. Choppy waves boiling like water waiting for spaghetti. I kinda like the me-against-nature feeling it gives me.

Beach deserted as I head for the packed sand at the shoreline. I veer right and fall into an easy rhythm, wind flipping my hair around like ribbons dancing.

My mind drifts like this: I think about SCRUBS. That makes me think of my guidance counselor with

his hairy knuckles. That makes me think of the
SCRUBS poop he shoved at me one day. SCRUBS.
Acronym (cool word) for **S**ummer **C**ollege-bound **Re**-
cruits **U**sing **B**rains for **S**cience. National search for
five outstanding graduated seniors to spend summer
in intensive pre-college medical training at prestigious
Fable Harbor University Hospital.

I thought: damn, that's a lot of superlatives.

I read it and I wanted it. Bad. Badder than that,
even. Who gets picked? Quote: "Candidates chosen
will be those five whom the selection committee feels
have the greatest potential to excel in a future medical
career."

Whatever that meant.

Application agony. Not a word to Anal Ree
LawSuit or The Skank lest they jinx it. Wanting so
bad I couldn't sleep. Only Erin-the-Body knew why.

Months pass. Slim letter in the box.

Read: Rejectionville, right?

Wrong.

Quote: "We are pleased to inform you that you
have been selected for the SCRUBS program, yada-
yada-yada."

And here I am on the beach. I stop, jog in place a
little, windmill my arms, and stretch my neck mus-
cles. I am going to work my butt off and be the best.
I'm going to prove that—

"Man, that dude must have a death wish."

A voice behind me. College Guy Heading For
Heart Attack By Forty smokes a filterless Camel as

his mutt runs circles around him, and cocks his head to the water.

"There's a surfer out there. Those waves gotta be, what, twelve footers? I figure, death wish."

I peer out at a figure on a surfboard. The waves have grown to ESPN proportions, and the sky is lead. Distant thunder booms over the crashing surf.

"Why doesn't he come in?" I wonder.

Heart Attack shrugs. "Got me. Here, Jordon! Let's go, boy, we're outta here."

Heart Attack and his best friend run off. My eyes stay on the surfer. He paddles down a monster wave and stands up. Holy Schlitz, he's riding it!!! He makes it look easy!!!

And I think: awesome. I want to learn to do that.

Suddenly he's gone, a lost blip on the radar screen of the ocean.

Where is he?

Where the hell is he?

Action proceeds thought, and I do not wimp out. I pull off my shoes and warm-up pants and launch into the suds, paddling powerfully, big rollers crashing over me, but I don't care. I'm nuts, but I'm at the area where he's gone down. I think.

I paddle in a circle gulping half air and half water. The violently teeming water is deadly now. It dimly occurs to me that I'm going to drown in saltwater just like my mother drowned in her own blood.

No flucking way. I'm too pissed to die. I won't fail the butt-hole surfer like I did Erin.

I'm gonna save his ass.

And then I'm gonna kill him.

And there he is. Bobbing twenty feet away.

"Hang on, I'm coming!" I fight the water with all my might, closing, closing, and then I reach for him, grabbing a fistful of hair.

He's screaming at me, but I hold on and yank an arm around his neck.

And then my eyes are on only one thing: the shore. Butt Hole thrashes around, screaming, and I punch him in the gut. "Stop fighting me, you idiot!"

And then we're standing waist-deep in the water, staggering toward shore.

"Are you insane?" he screams at me.

"I just saved your miserable life, you butt hole!" I yell back. I wipe half-hair half-seaweed from my face. "I should have let you drown."

"You are psychotic! I wasn't drowning!"

"Right," I snap back. "Look, just forget it, I saved you, I hate you, have a swell life."

"I wasn't drowning!" Butt Hole repeats, and the rain is driving now. "My strap broke and I was looking for my board!"

Butt Hole points at his right ankle. Bingo. Velcroed ankle band attached to two feet of rubber cord. I get it. The rest of the cord is attached to missing board.

I am such an idiot.

"Because of you, I just lost my best board!" Butt Hole rants. "Thanks a whole helluva lot."

"How the hell was I supposed to know?" I retort. "I live in Oklahoma!"

We stare in mutual fury.

"You're naked," he finally says.

"I am not." I look down. T-shirt. Panties. Soaking wet. Rendered transparent.

Not naked, exactly, but a walking one-woman wet-Tee contest.

Swell.

I look around for my jeans and running shoes. All I can see is rain.

And Butt Hole.

He's hot. Golden, sinewy athlete's body clad in soaked shorts. Electric blue eyes. Chiseled jawline. A walking dream. Currently a wet one.

Not that I care. Cute is meaningless. Guppies are cute, but they still eat their babies.

The rain lessens, and Butt Hole gets all excited because his board washes up fifty yards away. As for me, my clothes clearly are floating to Erin, so I'll have to walk back like this.

If I don't get arrested for indecent exposure along the way.

I push my lank hair out of my eyes when Butt Hole returns with said surfboard. "I can't say that it was nice to have met you, whoever you are."

"Right back 'atcha."

I say "Good-bye forever" and resolutely head for the street.

"You forgot 'and good riddance!' "

I shoot him the finger which is way juvenile but satisfying and keep walking.

When I reach the pedestrian path, he's beside me.

"Are you following me?"

"Don't flatter yourself. I left my stuff under that bench. Wait a sec." He takes a beat-up nylon back-pack from under the bench and pulls out a Hawaiian shirt and rubber flip-flops. He tosses them to me.

"Well?"

"Well, *what*?"

"Well, put them *on*." He sounds like he's speaking to someone mentally incompetent.

I hesitate. I deeply do not want anything of his, even temporarily. On the other hand, there is the almost-nude thing. The wind is making my nipples stand up and say howdy under my wet Tee.

He notices. I notice him noticing. I grab the shirt. And slip on the flip-flops.

I feel like a double dork.

"I'll wash the shirt and mail it back to you, with the flip-flops," I say in a voice I don't recognize as my own. "Give me your address."

"Forget it." He picks up his backpack, slings it over one shoulder, walks away.

I'm going the same direction. I trail him by twenty feet. We ignore each other. We both turn right, and then head up the hill. I pass him. We ignore each other some more.

Finally I turn back to him. "This isn't funny."

He barely glances at me. "That must be why I'm not laughing."

We both stop in front of the med school dorm.

"If you're a med student, here's a tip," he tells me. "Before you do something as stupid as what you just did, bone up on emergency medicine.''

"No need," I snap. "If you're the victim next time, I'll do humanity a favor and let you drown."

Open swings the door and I march up to the second floor. He's still next to me. I stop at my not-so-sweet suite. He stops opposite it.

> The five SCRUBS will form a cohesive team for the duration of the program, working, study-ing, and living together twenty-four hours a day. The women will share a suite in the med school dorm directly across from the men, and all five will take their meals together in either the med school or the staff cafeteria.

No flucking way.

I look at Butt Hole. "Are you—?"

He nods. "Don't tell me."

I nod. "I'm not turning cartwheels over this, ei-ther."

He sighs, reluctantly holds out his hand. "Tristan March."

I let his hand hang. "Zoey Appleton."

What else to say? He disappears into his suite, and I try my door, which I left unlocked. It's locked. I knock.

The door swings open. If *Female Perfection* mag-azine exists, the girl in my room is the FP poster girl. Long streaky wheat and gold hair that screams "I'm real!" Body by *Victoria's Secret*, face by Claudia Schiffer.

She makes Delia Lamont look like Tori Spelling.

FP adjusts her strand of perfect pearls and takes in the soaking Hawaiian shirt-clad mess who is me.

"Can I help you?" FP asks. Her drawl is barely north of Atlanta.

I go with disarming smile. "Hi. I'm your roommate, Zoey Appleton."

FP shrinks against the door as I slide by. "I'm Summer Everly."

"You look like a Summer Everly," say I.

The bed I'd claimed by the window is now made, and my suitcase is against the far wall.

"I moved your things," FP says, stating the obvious. "You hadn't unpacked yet."

"Then this really doesn't count as my soaking wet butt on your quilt" was my snappy comeback as I executed a perfect three-point landing on her bed.

Read: unexecuted three-point landing. Read: comment not made. Read: wimp out.

I hoist my suitcase onto the other bed and open it.

"Did you go out dressed like that?" she asks.

No. Please no. She's a younger, better-looking version of The Skank. I have jumped from mini-mansion frying pan into the not-so-sweet suite fire.

I contemplate flinging myself out the window. Decide I'd rather fling Summer.

Decide to go for the truth and live to tell the tale.

"I was jogging on the beach and I thought someone was drowning, so I jumped into the ocean in my underwear."

"Was someone drownin'?"

"False alarm." I rummage for an ancient Jimi Hendrix T-shirt, which reads ARE YOU EXPERIENCED?

FP's lips curl with amusement. "Just a little advice, Zoey," she drawls, pronouncing my name like it rhymes with the second word in the Chinese dish that starts with chop. "Next time you strip down to save someone who doesn't need savin', do it when you're wearin' cuter underwear."

Great comebacks flood my mind. None reaches my lips.

I grab clean clothes and take my underwear-clad self into the bathroom, slamming the door hard behind me.

So. Let's access, think I. I hate Tristan. I hate Summer. I hate my life. That about covers it.

I peel off my nasty not-cute underwear and decide to get over my pity party. I'm in Fable Harbor and I'm at Effing-Huh and I'm in SCRUBS. I'll work longer and harder than FP and Butt Hole put together. I will be the best. Go to Kenyon. Go to med school. Go home to Chaney.

Eye on the prize, Zoey-the-Mind. Indomitable me.

I decide I rock, and smile at my rocking reflection in the mirror.

My two front teeth are green with seaweed.

Neither Butt Hole or FP bothered to tell me.

2
TRISTAN

"Formaldehyde," I say, wondering at the same time whether there's anything as uncomfortable as the generic plastic chairs that populate every hospital cafeteria in the country. I've been in more than my share.

Who makes them, anyhow? Incarcerated felons?

I'm sitting across from my roommate for the summer, Chad Rourke, thinking how I lucked out. He's got a great sense of humor, knows when to talk and when to shut up, and he doesn't snore. Key qualities in a roommate.

"Don't tell me," Chad says. "Formaldehyde is 'good morning' in Hawaiian."

"A colorless gas used in solution to preserve dead bodies," I reply, as I check out the A.M. cafeteria scenery. Meds in white jackets, suits in suit jackets, worried families in Starter jackets. "And everyone in here looks like they've been dipped in it."

"Cheerful thought," Chad notes. "So how long before we take on the green glow of the walking dead?"

"Soon," I predict, taking a sip of my coffee. It tastes like warm sock juice. "Hospitals suck."

I take another sip of what passes for coffee while we wait for the SCRUBS orientation meeting to begin. What I'm really doing is imagining the surf. I was up before dawn and on the water until seven this morning. There's a big storm in the Atlantic, and the swells were outstanding. When I hit it right, ride it smooth and sleek, it's perfect, like great sex.

Which for some reason makes me think of that girl.

Zoey. Damn, but she's irritating. If my fave board hadn't floated in, I'd be even more irritated, but at least I got it back.

Stuck indoors for the whole summer with sick people and Saint Zoey. Shoulda known someone like her with a savior complex would be in this SCRUBS thing.

Chad spoons oatmeal into his mouth. "So, let me ask you, with an attitude like that, why are you here?"

"East Coast surf. Thought I'd check it out."

"You went through the endless bull to get into the SCRUBS program so you could leave Hawaii, surf capital of the universe, to come to Massachusetts and *surf*? Uh-huh."

I shrug. "Let's just say if this program had been

in Cincinnati, we wouldn't be having this conversation."

"You serious?"

Chad has this earnest streak to him. Seems like the kind of guy who never pretends to be too cool, which I like. What I don't like is talking about myself, so I just nod, and glance at my watch. Another ten minutes until Dr. Pace—whoever that is—comes to meet us SCRUBS.

"So, you all gung-ho to be a doctor, or what?" I ask.

Chad nods. "Sports medicine, I hope. How about you?"

I ask another question. "How'd you pick sports medicine?"

He smiles. "Honestly? A girl."

"Now, there's something I can relate to," I tell him, and it's the total truth.

"Eve Carrier." He says her name like it's a prayer. "See, in my neighborhood in Chicago, hoops are religion. I mean it. My parents own this tavern. Yack when the Bulls are on the tube, it's worse than farting at a funeral. You catch Jordan's last season? Awesome."

"No TV," I tell him. That's the total truth, too. In Alaska, Dad refuses to get a dish. No cable company wants to string a line three hundred miles to a village of one hundred Inupiat Native Americans and two white people. In Hawaii my mom used to have a TV, but she smashed it in an artistic hissy-fit when her former gallery dropped her. Never replaced it, either.

No biggie. I'm not a sit-in-front-of-the-tube kind of guy.

"B-ball's big in Alaska," I tell him. "Not much else for kids to do in winter."

"Well, it's big in Chi-town, too. I was desperate to play, but I was, like, five-two. Hadda settle for being the high school team manager. Eve was a physical-therapy grad student who worked with the team. I had this massive crush on her. So I pretended to be fascinated by P.T. so I could hang around her. And then, well, then I really did get interested in it. And I finally shot up seven inches, thank God. So here I am."

"Great story," I say. "So what happened to Eve?"

Instead of answering me, he kind of cocks his head to one side. "You play it real close to the vest, don't you."

I raise my eyebrows, but I know what he's talking about.

"Let's see," Chad muses aloud. "We're unpacking last night and you tell me your mom lives in Hawaii, your dad lives in Alaska, and you're a nomad between 'em. You hate being indoors and you love outdoor sports, the riskier the better, which probably makes you an adrenaline junkie. And that's the end of the Tristan March story."

"Maybe there's not that much to tell."

Chad smiles this friendly, disarming smile, and I find myself smiling back. I really like this guy.

"Now, why do I doubt that?" he asks.

I link my hands together behind my head. "Ya

busted me. Truth is, I'm in the witness-protection program, hiding from the mob."

"Excuse me, could I borrow your creamer?" says a breathy voice. It's attached to a young redheaded nurse who's all curves and dimples. Really cute. Absolutely my buddy Stevie's type. Ever since he fell in love with a red-haired girl in kindergarten, he's had a redhead thing.

I smile and hand her the creamer. Stevie definitely wishes he was here.

"Thanks." She flashes a grin back at me. "Are you, like, visiting someone here?"

"Nope," I say. "Are you?"

She giggles. "Lark Peyton. I'm a nurse."

"Tristan March, and your uniform was a dead giveaway." Her eyes are the same shade of auburn as her hair. Really wonderful. I cock my chin at Chad. "That's Chad Rourke."

"Hi," she tells him, but her eyes stay glued to mine. "So, if you're not visiting someone . . ."

"Summer med program," I fill in for her.

"*All* summer?" Lark asks hopefully.

"All."

"Great. I'll be seeing you, Tristan March."

"I'll look forward to it, Lark Peyton." I watch her walk away, taken by the beauty of that auburn hair as it swings with each step.

"Unreal. That happens all the time, right?" Chad asks.

"What?"

"What?" Chad repeats with a laugh. "She wants to clutch more than your creamer."

"Yeah?"

This cute blonde with a short haircut that emphasizes her beautiful neck walks by. She grins at me. I grin back. What a neck.

Chad folds his arms. "Okay, basically you're a babe magnet and I hate your guts."

"I plead guilty to liking women." I lean on the back legs of the ugly chair. "Short, tall, round, slim, young, old, they're just . . . they're all beautiful, some kinda way."

"Sorry, my man," Chad says, "but in the looks sweepstakes of life, everything female does not cash in a winning ticket."

"Not all in the same way, maybe." I look around the cafeteria, my eyes light on the woman two tables away. "Okay. See that lady over there? With the glasses?"

Chad looks over at her. She's reading the comics section of the newspaper. She's wearing a nothing-special pantsuit, has nothing-special hair, and probably weighs forty pounds more than she wants to.

"Yeah," Chad says. "What about her?"

"Watch her smile."

He looks at me like I just grew horns, looks back at her just as she reads a funny cartoon, and her face lights up like she'd been struck by the best kind of lightning.

"Nice," Chad admits. "But she's old."

I shrug. "One day we'll be, too."

Chad's looking at her differently now. "I read this article that said the best way to get introduced to the art of love is by an older woman."

"Yeah."

"What, you did?"

He's eager for info, but kiss and tell is definitely not my game so I just laugh.

"I can see it's going to be quite the experience being your roommate," he says. "I'll bask in the reflected glory and take notes."

"Hey, come on. You're a good-looking guy. Dark hair, blue eyes, athletic. I'm sure you do okay."

Chad shakes his head. "The truth is, in my head, I'm still the five-foot-two dork I used to be. Anyway, I'm the kind of guy that girls want as their bud. You're the kind of guy girls want, period. Must be fun. In fact, in my next life I think I'll come back as you."

"Beware of what you wish—"

"We're getting company," Chad interrupts me. By the cashier, Summer and Zoey are paying for their breakfasts. He shakes his head. "Now, those are two gorgeous girls."

We'd met Summer the night before when she'd knocked on our door with Zoey in tow. Zoey said zero to me, I gave her zero back.

I watch Summer walk toward us. By anyone's standards, she's world-class. She knows it, too. She's got on conservative gray pants and a thin white sweater and pearls, but she walks like someone just rubbed her down with baby oil. Calculated virginal do-me thing, Stevie would say. She fires up the cafeteria like the northern lights in December. Every guy's head spins to her, stripping her with their eyes. I bet a few of 'em mentally leave on her pearls just for yucks.

And here comes Zoey. Taller, leaner, darker, meaner. Baggy jeans and sneakers, hair up in a messy knot.

The un-Summer.

Steady. Fearless. Refreshing like a secret storm, like—

That's a lot of bull, Trist, I tell myself. *She's just a tall, irritating jock girl with a scowl on her face.*

"Good mornin', gentl'men," Summer says as she slides her perfect butt in next to me. Zoey plops down next to Chad and unloads her food from her tray. Lots of food. Summer has coffee and half a grapefruit.

"I see starting the program this morning doesn't have you too nervous to eat," Chad teases Zoey.

"Never happen." She takes a giant bite of a muffin. "I always eat like a horse. Sleep okay?"

"Nah," Chad admits. "Too excited about being here, I guess. Too worried I might blow the whole thing, too."

Zoey playfully bumps her shoulder into his. "You're gonna rock. I can tell."

Not a flicker of the eyes at me. Fine. We're in mutual ignore mode. I drain the so-called coffee.

"Did your missing roomie show?" Chad asks.

"Becky Silver," Zoey fills in. The names of all five SCRUBS are in our orientation folder.

"No sign of her," Summer chimes in, her voice all sweet southern honey. "I'm hopin' she never shows up at all. That alleged suite is too small for three people."

"Four," Zoey adds. "Your wardrobe takes up the space of another person."

Summer carefully blots her lips with her napkin. "A word to the clearly not-very wise, Zoey. People judge you by how you present yourself. You choose to present yourself like somethin' the cat dragged in, you'll get treated like somethin' the cat dragged in. I just happen to think more of myself than that."

Chad grimaces. "Yowza. Is it my imagination or did the temperature just drop ten degrees in here?"

"Zoey and I have not bonded like sisters, if that's your point," Summer says.

"Duh," Zoey adds. She takes a gulp of milk.

"Fine by me," Summer goes on. "I'm not here for a peejay party. I'm here to learn."

"Great," I find myself saying to her. "But you could chill out a little while you're doing it, don't you think?"

Summer fixes those feline eyes on me. "I was thinking more along the lines of heatin' up. How about you?"

Zoey makes a face. "Please, Scarlett, you're making me gag on rubber eggs."

Chad does a serious checkout scan from Summer to me and back to Summer again. "Unreal. You guys might be the two most perfect-looking people I ever saw in my life."

"Let's clone 'em, what do ya say?" Zoey suggests, and it's clear the thought does not entice her.

"I plan to remain an original," is Summer's cool reply.

"Listen, aren't there pills for someone with your personality disorder?" Zoey asks her.

Summer smiles. "Honey, gawky flat-chested brunettes like you would kill for a pill that would turn them into someone like me."

"Ooh. That's cold." Chad grimaces.

"Also not accurate," I add. "Zoey has decent breasts. I've seen her naked."

Zoey goes beet-red. "You have not."

"Good as," I say.

Chad looks at me. "Now, why does that not surprise me. You saw her—?"

"You are so—why are we talking about my breasts, anyway?" Zoey sputters. "We're here to study medicine, remember?"

"In that case, a little anatomy refresher shouldn't get your panties in a wad," I say.

"My panties are not in a—"

"I prefer G-strings, myself," Summer puts in.

Zoey slams her palms on the table and jumps to her feet. "The two of you and your massively oversized egos deserve each other," she says, steel-voiced. "I'm outta here."

"To where?" Chad asks.

"Orientation, obviously," she replies hotly.

"But Dr. Pace is meeting us here," Chad reminds her.

Down she sits.

Face bright-red. I smile to get her goat, but she won't be got.

Instead, she takes another bite of her muffin.

Dr. Pace, associate administrator of FHUH, has ankles almost as perfect as Summer's. Which are attached to the hard body of either an athlete or the gym-obsessed. I'm guessing the latter. Dark, straight hair. Icicle eyes.

She marches us out of the cafeteria and down the hall to a conference room, where she proceeds to demonstrate who's the toughest bear in the woods.

"The first thing I want you all to know," she says, "is that I think the SCRUBS program is a colossal waste of time and that I did everything in my power to prevent it from coming into being."

And the fun begins.

I look at the others to gauge their reaction. Chad and Zoey's jaws hang open. Summer is smiling. But I don't think she finds Dr. Pace funny.

Dr. Pace turns to check me out. I give her zero—I'm frozen like I'd be if she were a grizzly who just turned to look in my direction. She doesn't like it, I can tell.

She stabs her finger at the empty seat next to Zoey. "As for missing Ms. Silver, if she isn't here by the time our little session is over, this program will have one fewer intern than planned."

Summer's smile broadens a touch.

There's a knock on the door. I'm hoping it's Becky

Silver, so she won't get axed, but it's a guy. Mid-forties, graying hair, distinguished-looking.

"Oh, Dr. Bradley," Dr. Pace practically oozes in his direction. "SCRUBS interns, meet Dr. Peter Bradley, chief of hospital administration. He runs this place. Dr. Bradley, meet the physicians of tomorrow."

Talk about your about-face. She's got a serious Dr. Jekyll-Ms. Hyde thing going on.

Dr. Bradley beams like he just won the Iditarod. "Welcome to FHUH," he says. "And please call me Dr. B—everyone does around here. We're all *so* excited about the SCRUBS program. Especially Dr. Pace here. She'll help you any way she can."

Huh? Major intrigue with the higher-ups. I am so not interested in their games.

"I'm just prepping them for orientation, Dr. Bradley," Dr. Pace says, all pseudo-warmth and enthusiasm.

"Super. Well, I'll see you all later. Just wanted to introduce myself." Dr. B waves good-bye and closes the door behind him.

"Nice guy," Chad comments. Zoey nods in agreement.

I'm busy watching the icicles re-form on Dr. Pace. How she looked at Dr. B makes me think she's doing him.

Dr. Pace glares at Chad. "Do you plan to become a doctor, Mr. Rourke?"

"Uh, I hope so," Chad replies uneasily.

"Then learn to act like an intern. Doctors are busy

people. Time is precious, patients are waiting. Therefore, you do not talk unless asked to comment. Is that clear?''

Chad nods. Summer smiles. Zee-girl looks aghast.

Dr. Pace paces. "As you can see, Dr. Bradley is a big fan of SCRUBS. Fortunately, he had the good sense to put me in charge of it. So therefore, your fate this summer rests in my hands, and my hands alone. Am I understood?''

She is.

Dr. Pace looks at her watch. "One of the orderlies will be here in two minutes to take you on a tour. After that you'll work today in the hospital library reshelving books. As for Ms. Silver, she's about to be a scrubbed SCRUB. Good day.''

Dr. Pace strides to the door and nearly collides with the girl barreling through it. About five-four, golden skin, wild dark curls, not a straight line on her. She practically skids to a stop.

"Am I in the right place?'' the girl asks breath-lessly.

"I sincerely hope not,'' Pace replies. "Who are you?''

"Becky Silver,'' the girl reports. "Who are you?''

"Your boss. If I don't kick you out of the pro-gram.''

Becky's hand flies to her mouth. "I am so sorry that I'm late. I would've been here on time, but there was a taxi strike in New York and then the weather got bad and they canceled my flight and—''

She's talking to the air. Pace has marched out the door and shut it in Becky's face.

"—that's why I'm here today instead of yesterday," Becky tells the shut door. She slides into a seat and drops her head into her hands.

"The Virus strikes," Zoey quips.

Becky raises her head. "The who?"

"That was Dr. Pace," Zoey fills in. "Also known as The Beast of the East. Also known as The Virus."

"Since when?" Chad asks, laughing.

"Since I just made it up. Although I did read The Virus thing in a really funny book." She holds a hand out to Becky. "Hi. I'm Zoey Appleton."

"Becky Silver." They shake.

Chad introduces himself, then me and Summer. He's that kind of a guy. Most Likely to Be Nice, something like that.

Summer shakes blond locks off her face, eyes Becky coolly. "Dr. Pace was just about to cut you from the program. I'd watch my step if I were you."

"Great, she hates me," Becky groans.

"Hey, don't worry about it," Chad assures her cheerfully. "She hates all of us."

"Speak for yourself," Summer drawls. "She's goin' to be my mentor."

Zoey smiles. "Swell. The two of you can freeze-burn victims with your scintillating personalities."

The door opens again. Young guy, skinny, Asian-looking, wearing a white jacket and a backward baseball cap, bops into the room. "Hey, you guys must be the SCRUBS. I'm Leopold Seng. Call me Leo. No, no—no autographs, please.''

We all stare at him.

"It's a joke,'' he explains. "Not for long. Fame's gonna be my middle name. So, you ready to rock 'n' roll? The Virus told me to take you guys on a tour.''

Zoey gasps at this. "Wait. How did you know that's what I called her?'' She whirls around, staring at the ceiling. "Oh, Schlitz, are we secretly being videoed with one of those nanny-cam things? I am so f—''

Leo falls over himself laughing. "Take a breath. We all call her that. I think she likes it. So, we gonna boogie, or you wanna hear my DiCaprio imitation?''

3
TRISTAN

E-mail
To: tristmarch@juno.com
Fr: stevedaman@aol.com
Re: The waves you're missing, big guy

Tristan—

I steel can't get my mind around the fact that you took a surfboard with you to Massachsits. I here they have waves that are surfable about once ever sex years. Meanwhile, here on the north sure it's rocking four early summer. There were twelve-foot tubers and Billie broke a board and nearly broke her neck, but she's okie. As for me, I'm doing okie, you no me, never say die. That is a joke you cretin. Still hope to be riding the big won by the beginner of the year.

I figure with my double vishun I can now have twice as much fun at the beach. That is another joke. Thank God for this new voice recognizer on my computer. Look ma, no hands and I am righting to Trist. It is suppose to be ninety percent accurate but sum words come out funny as you can see. Maybe I am part of some big cosmic joke. If my vishun is bow cuss I can voice out your emails to me. So I'll just be DYING here, waiting for your noose. Ira checked in today which was cool. Keep laughing, dude.

Stevie

E-mail
To: stevedaman@aol.com
From: tristmarch@juno.com
Re: SCRUBS, Day One

Stevie—

Did you put in a special order so that your voice recognition system types "six" as "sex"?

Read your e-mail sex times. I still feel like a jerk for leaving you in Hawaii to come out here. I know you told me two thousand times in the last two months to get off my board and get on the plane to FHUH and okay, I did it. But if you need me and you don't let me know asap, I'll kick your ass. Fable Harbor is perfection. As is this SCRUBS beauty, Summer Everly. You'd drool. Better yet, change your treatment locale and you can zip out here and drool in person. FHUH has a kick-ass oncology unit—we toured through it today—very impressive.

So I'll give you the high points of day one. The head of the program, Dr. Pace, aka The Virus, reminds me of a frozen glacier—beautiful to look at, heart of ice. The other SCRUBS, besides the perfect Summer—my roommate Chad, a good guy from Chicago; Becky, a curvy dark beauty from New York, seems like a sweetheart. And Zoey. Nothing to tell there except that she almost drowned me before I even knew her name. Not worth going into. Guy named Leo took us on the grand tour of FHUH. He's Cambodian-American, works as an orderly until he can escape to Hollywood and become a star. He invited us to some bash at his beach house tonight.

Basically this place is medical city. There's a skywalk that connects hospital to the med school building, which connects to the research facility, which connects to the administration building, which connects to the psychiatric services pavilion, and the hipbone connects to the legbone.

The big tour: first floor, ER. Little kid came in on an ambulance with a wrist artery wound, the blood spurting out of him like a fountain. Chilling. Second floor, oncology. Excellent cure rate. And the ICU. Lotsa machines beeping.

The nurse's station is in the center of a huge open area so they can visually monitor all the patients. Third floor, ORs, transplant unit. Fourth and fifth floor: pediatrics. Peds is giant here. They've got beds for a hundred kids and they're full up. Intense. More on this later.

We never did get to floors six through eight, 'cuz Leo had to hustle us up to nine for our first crucial assignment. Reshelving books in the hospital library. No joke. If this is going to be the deal here, I'm not here for long.

Back to peds, where we hung out when Leo got paged for something or other. If you saw the preemies born addicted to crack and crank you'd want to put your fist through someone's face. This kid, Jerome Franklin, all of ten years old, with bone cancer and only one leg because they already amputated the other one. He flies around on his crutches and plays like he's a bad street dude even though both his parents are college professors. He takes care of all the little kids in the ward and makes 'em laugh. This kid might be even funnier than you. Cute little six year old, Kelly Markell, with brittle diabetes, climbed in my lap and stole my heart. She reminds me of Billie when we were kids.

Got really whacked by these twin guys our age, Shane and Rick Carr, with secondary pulmonary hypertension—out of control blood pressure from congenital heart disease. Really nice guys, hanging out waiting for a heart-lung transplant or death, whichever comes first.

There's lots more, but I'm still hoping to get you here so you can check it our for yourself. I hate to hear that your double-vision has gotten so bad that you can't type anymore, even though it ups the entertainment value of your e-mails. Knowing you, you'll program it so that some gorgeous female voice does the talking. Remember, if there is any change in the tumor, don't e-mail me. Call. Instantly. I gave you the number before I left. I'm e-mailing Ira not to forget you.

I'm pulling for you, Stevie. Trust me, when I was out riding the waves this morning, you were with me.

Tristan

4
ZOEY

I'm pulling on my second-favorite baggy jeans when underwear-clad Becky comes out of the bathroom. Red bra. Teeny panties ditto. Even her curves have curves.

Curve Envy strikes. I quickly discard it. I liked Becky from the instant I met her. Envy is unworthy.

"Where's Scarlett O'Hara?" Becky asks, rummaging through her suitcase. She hasn't had time to unpack yet.

"She made a point of telling me she was going over to Leo's with Tristan," I say. "Like I care."

As Becky unearths a long, gauzy, retro hippy-ish skirt, she says, "Honestly, I gotta admit, she fascinates me. It's like I hafta find out what makes her tick."

"I plan to stay far away from The Bad Seed, my-self."

Becky smiles. "Ya gotta admit, the girl is, like, out-there beautiful. And she must be smart, or she wouldn't have made it into this program."

"So?" I wrestle a blue shirt from the closet and slip into it. Sit cross-legged on my bed and watch her finish dressing. Sheer red blouse with rhinestone buttons. Matching lipstick. She piles her wild curls on her head and stabs them in place with colorful hairpins, but some hair falls down her back anyway. Dangly earrings.

She rocks.

"People interest me," she says. "The weirder, the better."

I draw my knees up. "In the burbs of Oklahoma City, Summer is not weird. There are endless Summers. Must be some kinda franchise thing goin' on for babelicious blond bitches. Triple Bs. Yeah. I like it."

"With brains," Becky adds.

"Quad Bs in her case. In the South, Triple Bs go forth and multiply and shall soon inherit the Earth." I shrug. "Trite. As opposed to you. I don't know anyone who looks like you."

Becky laughs her big laugh. "Yeah? What a hoot. I'm to New York what Summer is to the South, I guess. Every girl in Spanish Harlem looks just like me."

"That's where you live?"

"Yeah. Upper West Side of Manhattan." Becky

sprays herself with perfume. "Neighborhoods change from one block to the next. Harlem's black. Spanish Harlem's brown."

"You're Latina?" I guess.

"Please. Does Becky Silver sound Latina?" Her feet slide into strappy sandals.

"It sounds . . . Jewish, I think," I venture.

"They have Jews in Oklahoma?"

"One or two," I reply. "But they need a passport."

She laughs again. She has this great laugh. Full-bodied. "It's like this. My dad's Jewish and white. My mom's Baptist and black. My little brother and I ended up kind of caramel-colored. So everyone thinks we're Puerto Rican, but we're not. You ready to walk to Leo's?"

"Yeah, just let me grab a jacket." I do, grab my father's medical bag, which I use as a purse, and we're out the door.

While we walk, Becky talks. Her parents are both actors—stage, TV commercials, small roles in films. Artsy, bohemian childhood, play readings in her living room all night, that kind of thing.

Like I've a clue about that kind of thing.

Becky chose science over art. Got into Bronx Science (which she lets slip is this kick-butt school). Her parents cheered. They're still cheering.

She digs 'em.

Life Envy strikes. I try to discard. Fail.

I inhale the fresh night air deeply. "Smells like the ocean."

"Inhale like that in New York and you suck up someone's hubcaps," Becky says.

I laugh, suddenly feeling much better about everything. So what if we spent the day pushing books around? That'll change. So what if Tristan and Summer are loathsome? Becky and Chad are great. I'm on my way to a party. Far from The Skank and the burbs. What could be bad?

"So, you always want to be a doctor?" she asks me as we hit the beach and head east.

"Always. You?"

"When I got into Bronx Science, I was sure I was gonna be this astronaut."

"So what changed your mind?"

"My brother."

I question her with my eyes.

She makes a face. "Way too heavy to go into when we're on our way to our first party." She brushes back some curls that have come loose. "Anyhow, now I'm Miss Medical junkie, I swear. I am so psyched about becoming a doctor."

"Me too."

"To get to spend the summer here, doing medicine before we ever start premed . . . it's just awesome, you know?"

I do.

"I keep thinking about the scholarship," she goes on. "It's kinda great and at the same time it kinda sucks. I mean, it pits us against each other in a way."

The twenty-five-grand scholarship for the best SCRUB, she means.

The best. Which will be me.

"I really need it," Becky confesses. "My parents give love, support, art, and fun. Everything but money. Which they haven't got."

Boo-hoo. I don't have parents, says nasty Life Envy evil twin in my head.

Leo rents a house on the beach with two guys and two girls. He told us to walk east on the beach and stop at the last house before the pier. The purple house. Read: party central.

We hear cranked grooves way before we finally reach the purple. *So* purple. Day-Glo-colored rocking chairs on the porch. Tattered peace flag on flagpole. Under-twenties swarming like fire ants, partying in all usual ways.

"Hey, glad you two finally made it!" Chad calls to us from the crowded porch. A girl bumps him from behind, kisses him, then runs down to the beach with another girl.

"Friend of yours?" I ask him over the music.

"Never saw her before in my life." Chad shrugs happily. "Is this great, or what?"

"I love you!" This from a huge guy wearing an operating room mask as a hat careening toward Becky, arms outstretched. She feints to the side and he stumbles off.

"Please tell me he isn't a surgeon," Becky says.

"Mechanic," Chad fills in. "Larry something. One of Leo's roommates. You guys want beverage? Follow me."

Weave through the masses to the kitchen. A pretty,

slender girl who looks something like Leo tries to drown fruit punch with ginger ale.

"Hey, Tia, meet two more SCRUBS," Chad says.

She grins, wipes hands on her jeans, shakes ours. "Hi. I'm Tia Seng, Leo's sister. Someone emptied a fifth of vodka into the punch. I'm trying to dilute it."

Becky and I opt for warm Coke instead.

"So, welcome to Fable Harbor," Tia says. "It's a wonderful place."

Becky, leaning against the counter: "Did you grow up here?"

Tia nods. "Leo and I and our older sis Vic were all born at FHUH. My parents and grandmother think that when they left Cambodia they found paradise. They don't even like to go to Boston."

"What grade are you in?" I ask, guessing that she's around sixteen.

She laughs. "I'm a nurse. A floater."

I know what that is—a nurse who fills in wherever she's needed.

"No kidding?" Becky marvels. "I thought you were a kid, too."

"I'll take that as a compliment. Leo is my baby bro."

"Leo the future movie star," Becky says.

Tia shakes her head. "Asian actors get cast as hoods or martial artists. But Leo's a dreamer. He's the only one in our family who doesn't want a medical career. Our grandmother runs the volunteer program. Both of our parents are doctors. And Vic is head resident."

Chad grins. "Impressive. My folks own a bar."

Tia pours chips into a bowl. A guy with Frisbee-sized pupils snatches them from her, stuffing his face on the run.

"Herb-assisted munchies," Becky guesses.

"Probably," Tia agrees. "I thought my parents were going to spontaneously combust when Leo told them he was moving out and moving in here."

"Looks like a blast to me," Chad says as two girls in minuscule bikinis trot through the kitchen.

"My parents are strict. Very Cambodian."

"And I'm so American I make Donny Osmond look like a refugee," says Leo. He hops into the kitchen wearing movie-star sunglasses, doing a Travolta/*Saturday Night Fever* kinda thing sans white suit. "How goes it, lovely ladies?"

"It goes fine," I reply. "Nice party."

"We aim to please," Leo says, bowing. "Anything you need, drink, smoke, toke—"

"Leo!" Tia objects.

He throws an arm around her. "I'm joking!"

He's not. But she pretends to buy it.

"Got some hot tunes cranked," Leo says, eyes on Becky. "You look like a lady who can groove."

Becky laughs. "Are you for real?"

Leo dramatically unfurls one hand. Becky takes it. "What the hell, I'll live dangerously."

They go to dance. Tia asks Chad to dance, includes me, too, but I say I'll walk around.

I do, and it's a wild scene. Erin'd love this. No Tristan in sight. Not that I'm looking for him.

I walk back out to the beach. The ocean calls. I take off my sandals and sit in the sand, party sounds behind me.

"Hey."

Guess who. His voice doesn't sound like anyone else's.

"Hey back."

Tristan peers at the ocean. I stare at him. Look away when he looks again.

"Mind if I sit?" he asks me.

"Where's Summer?" I ask back.

He doesn't answer me. He sits, golden wrists dangling over hard-edged knees. "It's the sound," he says softly.

I know he's talking about the ocean. I nod.

"There's a rhythm to it. Like a mother's heartbeat."

Way too poetic. Is it Seduction Game Plan 101? Not that he'd want to seduce me. Not that I'd want him to.

He goes on, same voice. "There's this cliff-diving show on Oahu for the tourists. My friend Stevie lied his way into it when he was only fourteen. Guys dive eighty-five feet, straight down. No fear, he used to say to me. When his body cut through the water, even the silence had a rhythm to it. As long as he respected the ocean, he knew he'd be safe."

"Be sure to pass that cozy little tale on to the families of drowning victims, won't you?"

He doesn't rise to my fly. Which makes me feel semiguilty for cracking wise.

To make amends: "You're from Hawaii?"

"My mom lives there. Dad's in Alaska."

"That's quite the love commute."

He half-smiles. "They haven't loved each other in a long time."

He's being human. More than. Creating serious havoc with parts of my body that have never seen the light of day.

"I'm sorry about your surfboard" pops out of my mouth. Unbidden. Did I just say that?

"S'okay. I got it back."

"So you made me feel like Schlitz just for the halibut?"

"Like *what*?"

"Schlitz," I mumble, red-faced. "Halibut. I'm trying to curb my cursing habit."

"Halibut is a curse?" is all he says. Bemused. Vaguely superior.

Truly annoying. So I say, "I'm gonna learn to surf."

"You think?" He still sounds superior.

"I *know*. And believe me I wasn't hinting that you should teach me. I've seen you in action, and I'd like to live long enough to actually become a doctor."

He scratches his chin. There is the barest hint of stubble, glinting in the moonlight. "Way I figure it, the only moment we really have is now."

"Gee, deep."

"You're very annoying."

"Thank you."

He sighs. "Someone else teaches you, they'll mess

you up. Just remember: you don't follow directions, or you wimp out in the surf, your first lesson is your last. Got it?''

"I didn't ask you for lessons, remember?''

"Look, I can see that you're athletic. And graceful. You wanna learn, I can teach you.''

"Wait. Did you just *compliment* me?''

He shrugs. "Objective fact. You want the lesson?''

I hesitate. No fear. I nod.

He nods back. He smiles at me. Melting strikes.

My IQ drops. I'm thinking: remake the hot beach scene in *From Here to Eternity*, a fave Erin/Zoey rental classic. I wonder: what are the effects of sand in places that never see the light of day?

A cloud descends. It smells of orchid perfume. Summer.

"Glorious night, isn't it?'' she purrs, stretching so her perfect breasts strain against the sheer material of ankle-length summer dress.

"Having fun?'' Tristan asks her.

"Spiked punch and horny men lookin' to get lucky?'' she asks. "Did I shave my legs for this?''

From Tristan: "Did you?''

"You tell me.'' Her eyes lock with his. Slowly she lifts the bottom of her long dress. It clears calves. Knees. Silky thighs. And beyond.

Ick. I'm a prisoner at CAFE AU LAID. It's a strip show for one. Not me.

As the dress goes over her head: "I think I'll go for a swim.''

There's Summer. Truth in advertising. She really

does prefer G-strings. And Victoria's Secret under-wires.

She lifts her hair off her neck, lets it fall again, very calculated.

"Anyone care to join me?" she asks Tristan.

He's already on his feet pulling off his shirt. He looks down at me, like "Well?"

Right. The three of us. And my underwear is just as not-cute as it had been the day before.

"I'll be taking a big fat pass," I say, scrambling up from the sand.

"Suit yourself," Summer singsongs. She holds out a hand to Tristan.

He actually takes it. I hate him all over again.

They walk into the sea as I jog back to Party Central. Review every curse word in my colorful collection. Change no letters. Review again. I walk around to the side of the house where it's dark, don't know why.

Lick my wounded ego, maybe.

"I can fly-y-y-y!" someone yells.

I look up. A guy's hanging from an upstairs window, arms outstretched. I recognize a surgical mask masquerading as a hat. Larry something, Leo's roommate. Who cares.

"Hey, sweetheart, did you know I can fly?"

"Go for it, Superman," I call back. Polluted, I figure. Musta swam in vodka-laced punch.

"I love you," he bellows. "I friggin' love you!"

Swell. The Triple Bs of the world get the Tristans.

I get The Man Who Mistook A Surgical Mask For A Hat.

"Fluck love, Superman," I tell him.

"Don't say that! Everything is so beautiful. And I love you so much. Lemme prove it!"

I open my mouth for my next hostile comeback. It dies on my lips.

Larry has taken a swan dive from the window.

He lands on a pile of driftwood. A fat broken doll, drooling blood.

5

TRISTAN

Two hours later we're in the jammed emergency room, all us SCRUBS in our new regulation red SCRUBS scrubs. We might as well wear neon signs that say DWEEBS 'R' US. We wouldn't stick out more if they'd set us on fire. What mental midget came up with red?

Anyway. We're in the ER, holding hands, feet, heads, and whatevers of about a dozen people from Leo's party. Like Larry I-Wanna-Be-A-Birdy, they all slurped down party punch. Dr. Agonetti's pretty sure it was laced with acid. Really bad acid, too. These people are flying. Some of 'em literally.

One of the someones is Becky. They had to tie her down to a bed she got so nuts, screaming that she was going crazy, banging her head into the wall. I felt terrible for her. Zoey's in there with her.

So it seems that while Summer and I were getting up close and personal in the ocean, someone with a brain the size of a lentil decides to liven up Leo's party by spiking the punch with LSD. That crap sucks to begin with, and clearly this is a really bad batch of it.

The beauteous Summer and I are walking back to the party, I'm thinking how Summer seems cool even when she's hot. Like I'm kissing her, but I'm not kissing *her*. 'Cuz she isn't there. Her mind is outside of her body, watching.

I come out of this musing, realize the pounding music is no longer pounding. Then I notice red lights coming and going, coming and going.

Ambulances look the same everywhere.

Three of them are in front of the house loading victims of the punch. Number four is speeding to the ER with Larry. Zoey is mute, the color of a sailfish belly, twitching like she'd just been caught.

We follow the ambulances to FHUH. At the ER Tia tells us to get into our reds and get our asses back to the ER as fast as we can. The best thing to do for people on bad acid is to monitor them, make sure they're safe and just calmly be with them, hold their hand. The real pros get to monitor. We get to hold hands.

The guy I'm watching finally falls asleep, plus an official nurse's aide is with him, so I drift two doors down the hallway to see how Becky is doing. I knock, open the door slowly. Zoey is sitting next to Becky, holding her hand. The restraints are gone. Becky stares at the wall like she's watching Hannibal Lecter go for the guard in *Silence of the Lambs*.

"How is she?" I ask.

"Unfortunately, you'll probably find out any minute now," Zoey says, her voice low.

Suddenly Becky's head snaps upward. "No, Jake!" she screams. "Don't! Don't! Oh, God!"

"Don't what?" Zoey says, her voice as calm as she can make it, but quavering nonetheless. "Don't what, Becky?"

"Make him stop!" Becky screams. "Oh, Jakey."

Zoey strokes her hair. "Jake's okay, Becky."

Becky rips her hand from Zoey's. "Are you crazy? Can't you see? He's doing it again!"

"Who?"

"You have to stop him, Doctor! He's hurting himself!"

"Who's Jake?" I ask Zoey.

Zoey gives a helpless shrug. "She's been talking about Jake since I got here. But she won't tell me who he is."

Becky turns to me, livid. "You call yourself a doctor?"

"Uh . . ." I am at a loss for words.

"Do you call yourself a doctor?" she thunders.

Zoey and I look at each other, unsure as to what to say. I decide to play along. I can always press the emergency button and someone official will come running. Theoretically.

"What do you want to say to a doctor?" I ask her.

"That you suck," Becky says, a weirdly happy smile on her face. "Do you know how bad you suck?"

I hesitate. "We do," I say.

Tears rain down Becky's cheeks. "A twelve-year-old boy is smashing his head against the wall right behind you and you two so-called doctors aren't doing anything."

I look at the wall. I look back at Zoey.

Becky goes to the wall, Zoey follows. "I'm sorry, Jakey," she sobs to the wall. "I would help you if I could. But I'm just as crazy as you are." She turns her tear-filled eyes to Zoey. "Please, he's bleeding so bad."

"I'll help him," Zoey says. She grabs a towel and mimes stopping the flow of blood on someone named Jakey who isn't there. "Look, the bleeding is slowing down," Zoey says.

Becky shudders back her tears. "Is it?"

"Yes, it is. It's stopping, see? Jake's tired. He wants to lie down and rest."

"That's good, Jake. Rest now." Becky turns, shuffles back to the bed. She lays down, curls up in a fetal position. "Rest, Jakey," she murmurs, and closes her eyes.

Zoey sags against the wall.

"You were amazing just now," I tell her.

Her face lights up at the compliment. She looks about twelve. Utter guilelessness. I have this incredible urge to fold her into my arms. I take a step toward her.

The door opens. It's Tia with the beauteous one.

"How's our patient?" Tia asks.

"Sleeping now," Zoey says. "She had a really hard time, though."

"Poor kid," Tia says. "Larry Birdy is going to be fine. Two broken wrists, contusions, lacerations, and a very bad headache."

"Thank God," Zoey says fervently, closing her eyes. I'm surprised at her impassioned reaction.

"Yes, he's very lucky that—" Tia's beeper goes off, she looks at it, curses, heads out the door.

Summer checks out Becky, her face blank. "It looks like most of the drug has passed out of her system," she says dispassionately. "No more trying to bash in her own head, I see."

Zoey shakes her head. "That's a helluva bedside manner you've got. She's your roommate, remember?"

Summer doesn't flinch. "Here's what I see. Patient is an eighteen-year-old female Latina, slightly overweight, vitals good, currently stable and resting comfortably."

"She's not Latina," Zoey snaps.

"I know that," Summer shrugs. "But when a patient is incommunicado, a doctor assesses by observation."

"Last I heard, compassion was still part of medicine," I say.

Summer turns to look at me for the first time since she came into the room. There's zip on her face to acknowledge that a few hours ago we were becoming intimately aware—visually anyway—of the usually-clothed parts of our respective bodies.

"Well, I'll just have to write that little homily down, Tristan," Summer drawls, "so I can pass it on to the department of neurosurgery."

"You know, you are one cold bitch," Zoey says.

Summer smiles. "And you have the backbone of a tampon. Right now Becky is a patient. But you, Zoey, won't treat her like a patient. Which means you can't help her. I'm picturing some crisis, Zoey. Some friend or relative of yours is rushed to the ER. What does Dr. Zoey see? Not patient. Friend. When push comes to shove, my money's on you, Zoey, to shatter like the thin glass you are."

Zoey's face drains of color. She takes a step backward as if Summer had slapped her cheek.

"Zoey—" I begin. What will follow that, I don't know. But I do know that I can't stand to see her hurting.

But I don't get to say anything else. Because she runs out of the room. Literally. Runs.

"Now, what was that all about?" Summer wonders.

"Beats me," I reply, which is the truth.

Summer's face goes foxy. "Methinks I struck a nerve."

"Methinks thee looketh a little too happy about it."

I can almost see the wheels turning in her beautiful mind.

"Hmmm" is her enigmatic comeback. "Well, I'm

off. When's the next time we're going to have an *en masse* drug overdose to study?'' She nods at me and floats out the door.

Like we're strangers. And maybe we are.

It's two days later, Becky is back to normal. She hasn't asked about what she said or did under the influence. Well, at least she hasn't asked me.

We're spending the day in pediatrics. The little kids are the only ones at FHUH who like our reds. Got to trail rounds with head of pediatrics, Dr. Davis, and his summer interns. They stop at each bed and talk about each patient. Kelly Markell went into insulin shock last night, she's still feeling pretty punky. They're changing Jerome's chemo drugs. A thirteen-year-old heartbreaker in a junior Audrey Hepburn–Gwyneth Paltrow mold got readmitted. Named Amie. Malignant brain tumor. Her smile could power Fable Harbor.

As Davis reviews each presenting illness I hear the definitions in my head before he gives 'em. Sometimes he questions the interns. Sometimes they even know the answers. I keep my mouth shut.

Mostly, Davis ignores us. I can't say I blame him. He's one of the best pediatrics specialists in the country—thousands of med students apply to work with him. All he needs are five kids dressed in red scrubs trailing him like a moving blood clot in a crucial vein.

If I were him, I'd ignore us, too. In fact, much of the time, my mind's far away. With Stevie in Hawaii, his back propped against an outrigger turned on its side, watching not surfing. Or in the Brooks Range, on a caribou hunt.

Not indoors with the sick, dying, dead.

Last night Chad asked me for maybe the tenth time, "Why are you here, man?"

For the tenth time I didn't answer him.

Rounds end. I hang with Jerome a little while. The kid gets straight A's in a gifted program even though he's missed weeks of school. But he talks like he's street. I try not to laugh. He has a green handkerchief hanging from the back pocket of his baggy jeans, tells me it's his gang's color. Wants to know if I can sneak adult videos into the ward. And women. He wants women. He tells me his last girlfriend was fifteen.

The radiant nurse, Lark, the redhead Stevie should marry, takes Jerome off for a spinal tap. They hurt like hell. Jerome bops on his crutches like he's heading to a party. The kid's unreal.

I walk down to the youth lounge. On the far side of the lounge, which boasts a big-screen TV, air hockey, and four computers, Becky sits with one of the Carr twins—the two guys waiting for heart-lung transplants. There's not a lot of personal space between them. Becky keeps nodding at whatever it is that the guy is saying. She puts her hand on his arm and nods again. Either she is a touchy person because she comes from an ethnic background, or I'm watching the germ of a thing they have for each other.

It's sweet.

I turn to leave, but Becky waves me over. As soon

as I'm up close, I know she's with Rick. No scowl, à la his twin bro, Shane.

"What's happening?" I say, sitting next to Rick.

"Oh, you know, not much," Rick says breezily. "Waiting for a compatible heart and lung donor, or waiting to die, whichever comes first."

"Hilarious," Becky says, hitting him on the arm.

Rick grins, hooking his pinkie with hers. "I'm in one of my black-humor moods. Never know what will come out of my mouth."

"The unexpected thrills me," she assures him dramatically. "Hey, Tristan, want to hear something amazing? When Rick and I were little, we both decided on becoming astronauts." Said as if to confirm that she and Rick are destined for each other. Becky and Rick. Rick and Becky.

I see it shining from their eyes.

"Ever read *Rocket Boys*?" I ask them. "True story of this poor kid—"

"Who builds a rocket from like, nothing," Rick fills in eagerly. "It's so great. I've got the movie—"

"*October Sky*, right?" Becky asks. "I never saw it."

"I could pop it in the VCR after dinner," Rick says, way casual. "But you probably have plans—"

"No, no, I don't," Becky assures him, quicker than quick. "I'd love to watch it with you. I'll nuke some popcorn at the nurses' station."

"No salt," Rick reminds her, rolling his eyes. "They check my sodium levels down to the fifteenth decimal point."

"No salt." Becky turns to me. "Want to come?"
I shake my head no.

Rick regards Becky. "You are one fast girl. We're about to spend our first night together in bed."

"Hey, Rick, did you take my cassette out of the cassette player?" It's Shane, rolling toward us in a wheelchair. Which means he's too weak to walk. Which could well explain the nasty tone of his voice.

"Haven't seen it," Rick replied.

"Well, who did, then?" Shane demands. "It's gone."

"Did you ask the nurses?" Becky suggests.

Shane fires off a withering look. "My heart is effed up, not my brain, okay?"

"All righty," Becky says good-naturedly. "I'll take that as a yes."

"Hey, Becky's gonna hang with us tonight and watch *October Sky*," Rick tells Shane.

"Nice of you to run that by me," Shane snaps.

"I'm running it by you right now."

"Maybe we can use the VCR here in—" Becky begins.

Rick touches her hair. "Don't worry about it. I'll work it out."

They're lost in each other. Shane goes caustic and rolls off into the sunset. I mumble something or other and take my leave. Becky and Rick never notice.

I walk down the hallway, checking things out. Summer's in the playroom, sitting in one of those awful orange prison chairs that must have migrated up from the cafeteria. Kelly Markell sits on her lap.

Two other kids, littler than Kelly, sprawl on the rug at her feet. One of them has an IV tube going into her arm.

Summer is reading to them from a book whose title I can see. *Zink the Zebra: A Special Tale.* Summer looks as glorious as a human could look in shapeless red. She doesn't notice me. Neither do the kids. I lean against the doorframe and listen.

"Zink was a normal zebra in every way. She had four legs, two ears, one nose, one mouth, one tail . . . and spots."

These kids have their eyes locked on Summer like she's Santa Claus. She's totally into it. Kelly's pressed up against her like Summer is momma bear and will protect her from whatever evil might come.

God, I wish adults could really do that for little kids. That Summer could do that for Kelly.

Summer looks so un-Summer, sitting there.

I slip out and practically crash into Zoey striding by. We haven't really talked since the Becky freak-out. Not about anything not medical, anyway.

"Hey," I say.

She heys back but barely slows.

"Zoey," I call. I don't even know what I'm going to say.

She turns around, waits.

I walk to her. "I was out surfing this morning before breakfast," I tell her. "There were three-footers, pretty good to learn on. I've got the longboard waxed. You ready for a lesson after work?''

''No. I'm busy.''

I can't imagine what with, since her schedule is my schedule.

''You sure?'' I ask.

''I already hooked up with a different teacher, actually,'' she tells me.

I'm surprised that I care. But I do.

''Thanks, anyway,'' she adds. Then she heads off to wherever she was heading in the first place.

Summer comes into the hall, stretching out her back.

''Pretty impressive in there,'' I tell her. ''I heard you reading.''

Her face gets guarded.

''Those kids were ready to eat fried worms if you asked them to,'' I tell her.

''I like kids more than I like adults,'' she says. ''It's too bad they have to grow up.''

''Around here some of 'em don't,'' I point out as we head to the teen lounge.

''FHUH has an excellent cure rate in pediatric oncology. In fact, the unit is world-famous.''

''That so?''

She nods. ''Dr. Beth told me a long time ago.''

''Dr. Beth?''

''My mentor.''

I wait to hear more but she isn't talking. We dodge around a gurney that two orderlies are wheeling off to surgery and come to the teen lounge.

"I was supposed to meet Dr. Davis here," Summer says, since he clearly is absent.

"Davis who hates us?"

She ignores this. "He's lending me an excellent book on pediatric psychosomatic disorders."

"From his personal library?" My voice is heavy with insinuation.

"Why, Tristy," Summer purrs at me. "You're not jealous, are you?"

I don't answer, but if I did the answer would be no. Jealousy is something I've never understood.

"Powerful men are powerful," Summer says. "Latchin' on to power is how you get power."

"What if you don't want power?"

Summer laughs. "You are the funniest, Tristan. Everyone wants power. Power makes the world go 'round. Sit and wait with me, we have a break until four." She sits and pats the spot on the couch next to her.

"I want to hear about Dr. Beth," I tell her.

"Tia Seng, line five, Tia Seng, line five," the intercom interrupts our barely begun conversation.

"I guess she's pulling another double," I note.

"Tia's good. Too bad she's utterly wasting herself on nursing. Dr. Beth worked fourteen hours a day, every day," Summer confides.

I nod, gazing out the floor-to-ceiling plate-glass windows that face the ocean mere blocks away. I wonder what would happen if a hurricane came rumbling up the coast. It'd be glass confetti in here.

Summer stares out, too. When she speaks again, her voice is far away. "The first time I saw Dr. Beth I thought—dang, she's so tall and ugly. Why doesn't she do something with that hair? It was only later on that I realized how beautiful she is.

"She took over for my family doctor in Tennessee when he retired," she went on. "She grew up on the Cumberland Plateau, too. That's—"

"Middle Tennessee, between Nashville and Knoxville," I fill in, just to shock her. "Rises from Nashville to Cookville to Crossville, then on to Knoxville, where—"

Summer laughs. "Tristan March! I'm impressed."

I smile. No need to explain myself.

"Dr. Beth Russell," she says. "Country doctor. She'd take me to Cookville General and let me play with the kids on the peds ward. I'd read to them. And it was just . . . it was perfect there. Dr. Beth loved me. I loved her. And she didn't take crap from anyone."

I laugh. "Sounds like quite the lady."

"You don't know the half of it," Summer says, looking out at the ocean again. "Not the half of it."

Finally it's the end of the day and all I can think about is hitting the beach, when my beeper goes off. All us SCRUBS now have beepers. I stuff the hideous reds into my locker and check the page. It's from Dr. Pace's office. Why she'd want to see me, I don't know.

I could go over in my scrubs or go over in the jams and T-shirt I was about to grab from my locker.

With The Virus, no contest. I pull the detestable reds back on, lace my Filas, and hurry out of the locker room, heading for the administration building.

I have this feeling that The Virus is at her desk, stopwatch in hand, ready to tell me that if I'm not there in less time than the current world record for the one hundred meter dash, I might as well go back to Hawaii.

Like I could care.

Outside, the ocean air hits my face, and I feel free for the first time since I walked into FHUH that morning.

My pass gets me into the administration building. I take the elevator up to the executive suite, where the main cheeses of FHUH city ripen and rot.

The receptionist points me to Dr. Pace's office, and my watch tells me it has taken me less than four minutes from the time of my page. Good enough, I think.

Dr. Pace's office is the second from the end. The one at the end belongs to Dr. Bradley.

I'm just about to knock on Pace's door when Dr. Bradley's door opens.

But it's not Dr. Bradley who exits the office.

Out steps Summer.

She's smiling like the cat that just ate the steak on the counter. And two sausages as a chaser.

She sees me seeing her.

Her lip curls.

And—this is the God-honest truth—she *winks* at me.

6

ZOEY

Dear Erin-ze-Corps,

Loved card from Paris. Loved kiss prints all over the Eiffel Tower. Love how you and Christof are en route to villa in south of France. For real?? Better be, as I'm sending this to said villa. Take photos. I want proof.

So. After ten days my feelings are mixed. Read: medically, beyond exciting. Got to see open-heart surgery. Ditto baby being born. Both awesome. Not awesome: how homeless and hopeless make hospital waiting rooms their home and hope. Take Zelda. A regular. Could be fifty, maybe eighty. Life in a shopping cart. Has wig wardrobe, comes in as a blonde one day, redhead next. All wigs equally trashed. Lives in women's shelter, says it's boring. Knows every word to "Bye Bye Miss American Pie." Tia sings with her.

On personal front, Okie sistuh is still in search of a life. Becky is a good friend. Chad, too. Summer is a Triple B cubed. And Tristan—I told you about him when you called—is still Tristan. Read: so hot he could melt ice. Read: so annoying I want to smack him and feed him to Zelda for dinner. He and Summer are a thing, I think. He doesn't say, I don't ask. Only to you, Okie sistuh, will I admit dreams about him so X-rated they'd be banned in OK.

Girl parts have no conscience.

Sinced you asked, I've still got big probs with insomnia. Late late late-night walks on the beach. Beats walking in Belle Woods any day. Or night.

Today I'm in ER. Exciting and scary. Call from the villa. Do everything *I wouldn't do.*

Love ya Okie sistuh,

Zoey-the-Mind

I seal aerogram and address it. Clearly, Erin's shoulder wound is not holding her back.

Check watch. Same time it said fifteen minutes ago. Check nightstand clock. Schlitz. My watch stopped and I'm late. No wonder no one's around. I sprint to the ER nurses' station, posting Erin's letter on the way.

Everyone's gathered around Leo's oldest sis, Dr. Victoria Seng, a.k.a. Head Resident a.k.a. The Anti-Virus a.k.a. The Kind Of Doctor I Want To Be. She listens. Treats patients with respect. Acts like we SCRUBS have working brains.

Dr. Vic reads a chart, reviewing a case for two med students and the SCRUBS. I sneak in hoping she doesn't see I'm late.

"The patient is Ms. Arlette Bacon. Fifty-eight years old. Undomiciled. Suffering from cellulitis. Can any of you tell me what that is?"

Behind us, two nurses share a look. Read: withering. Like, why is Dr. Vic wasting time on us? A common Effing-Huh sentiment. We rank somewhere under janitorial services in the Effing-Huh pecking order and get pecked appropriately.

Tristan notes the look, too.

"An ulcer resulting from the buildup of interstatial fluids, usually due to an impaired vein which improperly diverts blood flow from the heart," he says.

Jaws drop. Including nasty nurses'. All med students. And mine.

Dr. Vic is impressed. "That's correct, Mr. March. And 'interstatial' means—?"

"Between the cells," Tristan replies.

Dr. Vic nods. "Correct again. Ms. Bacon is in

Room Two. If you would follow me, please."

Summer to Tristan, as we walk: "Well, well. Now I know where you've been on those nights you haven't been with me. Squirreled away somewhere readin' medical textbooks."

No reply. Which is so annoyingly Tristan.

We walk into Room 2 (read: 9' × 9' examining module). Gray-haired woman on bed, hair wild, face slack. Nurse's aide nearby exercising Bazooka. On the floor, gray-haired woman's malodorous right shoe and sock.

The ulcer on her ankle is the size of my hand. Pus. Blood. It's pulsing. Maggots? Becky gags and I force myself not to look away.

"Good morning, Ms. Bacon," Dr. Vic says.

The woman, suspicious: "I don't know you."

"I'm Dr. Seng."

"Usually I see that nice doctor. The fat one."

"You mean Dr. Agonetti? He's not on duty now. Is your leg hurting you again?"

"Your jackets are ugly."

Becky laughs. "I agree with you."

Dr. Vic shoots Becky a please-shut-up look and then turns her attention back to the patient.

On Becky's blush. "Ms. Bacon, as this is a teaching hospital, may these students observe?" Dr. Vic asks.

A brief wary nod.

"We're going to keep your leg elevated, Ms. Bacon, and drain the wound. Medication indicated?" Dr. Vic asks the med students.

"Uh . . . adult diphtheria-tetanus toxoid?" the shorter ventures nervously.

"And also—?" Dr. Vic asks.

The students suddenly find the floor intriguing.

"Human tetanus immune globulin," Tristan offers. "Thiamine. Antibiotics."

"Very good, Mr. March," Dr. Vic intones. The med students stare hate daggers at Tristan.

Dr. Vic pats Ms. Bacon's arm. "Someone will be in shortly to tend to your leg. I'll be admitting you for a few days."

"That other doctor never admits me. I can't pay," she says.

"Don't let that worry you, we'll find a way. I hope you feel better soon, Ms. Bacon."

We ducklings follow momma back into the hall. Dr. Vic hands Ms. Bacon's chart to a nurse. "All yours, Michelle."

Michelle, underwhelmed: "Again? She's been here six times in the last three months." She sighs and heads for Room 2.

"I'd appreciate it if you'd clarify somethin' for me," Summer asks Dr. Vic. "Dr. Agonetti says we try not to admit a reepie unless the situation is critical."

Reepie is Effing-Huh slang for Repeater a.k.a. YY a.k.a. Yo-Yo a.k.a. Gomer a.k.a. Get Out Of My Emergency Room!

"Clearly this woman can't take care of herself," Summer says. "And clearly she'll just be back again. It doesn't seem cost effective."

"Please refer to all patients by their names, Ms. Everly," Dr. Vic says.

Summer blinks. It's a moment.

"Now, with Ms. Bacon," Dr. Vic continues. "It's a grave error to send someone home who should be admitted. Ms. Bacon has no home. This makes it difficult for her to keep her feet dry and warm. Which means that if we do not clear up her cellulitis at this stage, she will return shortly in worse shape than she is in now. Which would require a longer admission and more assertive treatment. Which would, in the long run, not assist her. Which would not be, as you put it, 'cost effective.' "

My infantile joy at Summer's momentary humiliation is boundless as Momma Duck leads us to Room 5.

"This patient is Angela Cowen," Dr. Vic reads from a chart. "She is nineteen and was admitted complaining of severe headaches and double vision."

"Possible brain tumor," the shorter med student pipes up. Read: eager beaver after floor-staring embarrassment.

Dr. Vic nods. "You did the uptake on Miss Cowen, Mr. Pratt, so please present." She hands him the chart.

"Miss Cowen is nineteen, a college student, previously in excellent health," Pratt squeaks. "She does not use drugs or alcohol, says she did not receive a blow to her head, and has no known exposure to . . . uh . . . toxins."

Dr. Vic, impassive.

"She ... uh ... takes no medications, eats what she described as a very healthy diet, and takes vitamins. Um ... I noted that her lips are cracked, and also she has some acne on her forehead and chin. In addition to the headaches and double vision, she complains of pain in the ... uh ... long bones of the body."

"Recommended course of action?"

"Uh ... CAT scan?"

"Before that?"

"Uh ..." Pratt gets psyched about the floor again.

"Mr. Frank?" she asks Med Student #2.

Zippo.

"Anyone?"

Flashback. In my mother's office. She's gently telling a mother the tests she wants to do to diagnose a little girl with terrible headaches and double vision.

"Test her reflexes," I say, my heart pounding. "And check for papilledema."

Dr. Vic looks at me. "Which is—?"

"Optic nerve swelling. It could indicate a tumor."

"Excellent, Ms. Appleton."

Thanks, Mom.

I swear I hear "You're welcome."

Room 5. Dr. Vic asks permission for us to observe, then begins her examination.

There's swelling of the optic nerve. Palsy of the fingers.

Becky and I share a look. We're thinking brain tumor. This girl is our age. In college. Could *be* us, in fact. God. Dr. Vic orders a brain CAT scan, and

Leo's right there with a joke to wheel her upstairs.

The girl is scared Schlitz-less.

Numb when Dr. Vic sends us to lunch. Summer takes Tristan's arm. How proprietary. Then she takes Chad's arm, too. *Ménage à trois. Comment chebran.* The three of them stroll off to eat whatever.

"Is that as icky as it looks?" I ask Becky.

"What, you think she's doing Tristan *and* Chad? Get out of here! Let's grab something and go eat outside, huh?"

Hit cafeteria. Veg out in endless line. Take food into sun-dappled courtyard. Full of green-tinged Effing-Huh personnel in search of sun-dappling.

"This food reeks, huh?" Becky bites into a mystery-meat sandwich.

"I can eat anything as long as there's lots of it." I chomp down massive amounts of fries, guzzle my Coke, begin to revive. Turn face to sun. Dapple.

Becky, with her face raised to the sun: "Deelish. I'll have to bring Rick down here some afternoon."

"You manage to work his name into every other sentence."

"No way."

"Every sentence, then."

She puts down mystery meat. "Okay, I'm busted. I'm telling you, Zoey, he's . . . well, he's great."

I chomp another fry. "Why don't I think that's a medical opinion?"

She smiles. "Yeah, I like him. A lot. Can you even imagine going through what he and Shane are going through? But he has this amazing attitude—"

"—Which makes you want to jump his amazing bones."

"Oh, right. Up in his room in the pediatric ward. While his brother, who also happens to be his room-mate, takes home videos of it," she says, laughing.

"You give me the word, I'll take Shane for a long roll around the hospital grounds, give you two some privacy."

"I have a feeling gettin' bootie is a little strenuous for the guy until after his transplant."

"Especially with you," I joke.

"Well, yeah," she agrees, laughing. She's the best thing since Erin.

Her face goes all solemn. "I keep thinking how lots of people die waiting for organs, you know?"

I do.

"Rick and Shane already decided that when a do-nor is found they'll flip a coin to see who gets the transplant."

"Schlitz," I say.

"No kidding. Schlitz. How do you deal with that, heads I win, my twin brother dies? Or the other way around?"

Don't know. Can't imagine. Would I save Anal Ree before myself? Beats me.

Becky draws knees to her chin, wraps arms around them. "I keep asking myself: if it was me and my brother, what would I do?"

"I was asking myself that, too."

Becky stares at nothing. "I don't think I could live if it meant Jakey would die."

Jakey.

A twelve-year-old boy is smashing his head against the wall right behind you . . . he's bleeding so bad . . . I'm sorry, Jakey.

My eyes slide to Becky. No reaction. When we'd talked about her involuntary LSD voyage, she hadn't remembered squat. Which meant she didn't know I know. Whatever it is I know.

"Becky," I say slowly, "when you were skydiving compliments of the Leo punch—"

"I'd love to know what asshole did that—"

"Me, too. You kept talking about a boy smashing his head against the wall. You called him Jakey."

Zing. Her face goes from guarded to caught to despair, just like that. Courtesy of *moi.*

"My brother . . ." She falters.

"You don't have to do this."

"I know." She's watching two birds flapping in the fountain, but she isn't seeing pigeons.

Her voice is flat. "Jake is four years younger than me. The sweetest, nicest, smartest kid. He inherited our parents' talent, not me. And he was so funny.

"So, I started Bronx Science and the science genius thing. Jakey was ten then, I guess. He stopped smiling, that's the thing I remember. Stopped doing homework. Didn't hang with his friends. If you asked him about it, he'd snap at you. My parents figured it was a stage, you know. And we were all so tight, they could just love him through it."

She tightens her arms around herself.

"I was sixteen, all caught up in working on my aeronautics project for the science fair with my friend. We thought for sure we could take the state, maybe even nationals. I was pissed off because my parents were shooting a film so I had to go home and make Jake dinner. I walk into the apartment and it's dark. But I hear noise in the bathroom, so I go in there. There's Jake. Smashing his head against the mirror, screaming at someone who isn't there. There's blood everywhere. I can't make him stop."

I reach for her hand. What else to do?

"They diagnosed him as a chronic acute schizophrenic. Tried every medical protocol there is. Nothing helped. We never knew when he was going to hurt himself. Once he set himself on fire. Another time he carved up his arm with a razor. Because the voices told him to do it."

She gulps. "My parents had to institutionalize him. The place he's in is nice, in upstate New York. It's no hellhole. Sometimes when I visit him, he even knows that it's me. He begs me to take him home."

Two fat tears roll groundward.

"I'm so sorry," I say.

"Me, too." She fists the tears away, pulls it together. "Look. I have a game plan. I'm gonna be a psychiatrist, specialize in severe mental illness." She shrugs. "Anyone can be an astronaut. But my little brother is a prisoner of his mind now. Maybe I'm the only one who can set him free and bring him home."

Bam. A fist into my heart. I could join the confessional. "My parents were killed in the Oklahoma City bombing" is how I would begin.

I don't.

I respect her pain too much to dilute it with my own. I reek of nobility. Read: Schlitz for bulls.

Soul-bearing is not my long suit. And I OD'd on platitudes four years ago. We sit. Holding hands. And I hope it's enough.

That night I can't sleep. Not unusual. I tiptoe out and head for the beach. Each wave seems to have a name.

Mom.

Dad.

Jake Silver.

They rush to me with open arms. There one moment. And the next, gone.

7
TRISTAN

Pace paces. A scowling Virus is amongst us.

All us SCRUBS are in our reds, and she's strutting around the conference room like a bull moose in heat. An expensive designer pantsuit is visible under her white coat. Her beauty is by-the-book and encased in ice.

Utterly unappealing.

We haven't seen much of The Virus, which is clearly how she likes it and how we like it, too. Various doctors shuttle us through various departments of the hospital. The Virus rears her membrane once a day, if that. It always seems accidental. She's always irritated. With us, anyway.

And now here we are, for our "evaluations."

Whatever that means.

No one says a word.

"So," The Virus speaketh, mid-pace. "Let's make this quick. I've got a busy day. Dr. Bradley suggests that some feedback from you would be *helpful* at this two-week point."

Her spin on *helpful* raises sarcasm to a high art form. She folds her arms, stares at us.

"Comments? Questions? Concerns? Suggestions?"

I sense bear trap. But Chad the Ingenuous plunges right in.

"I think the SCRUBS program is great," he says.

The spider Virus stares at him, a bug in her web.

"Really great," he adds lamely.

Oh, bad move, buddy. Hooking a state record arctic char with your flyrod is great. So tell her SCRUBS is instructive, a remarkable experience, eye-opening maybe. Not "great." Nor "really great." Not to The Virus.

The spider Virus sucks the life from the Chadbug.

"Does anyone have anything *articulate* to contribute?" Pace asks.

Zoey goes to raise her hand, thinks better of it, scratches her ear instead.

Me, are you kidding?

Summer, are you kidding?

"Fine," The Virus says. "It's been illuminating. Now, I have your two-week evaluations to—"

Summer's hand goes lazily skyward. Look at that! She waggles her index finger to get Pace's attention.

"Yes?" The Virus asks, interrupting herself.

I'm floored. Yeah, Summer said that Pace was going to be her mentor, but I haven't seen anything close to that developing. Let's see how the human cytomegalovirus reacts.

"Dr. Pace," Summer drawls easily, "we were all very impressed with our time on the pediatrics floor."

This is true. It was a group fave.

"Your point?" Pace asks, warmth-free.

"We formed relationships with many of those young patients," Summer flows. "We'd like to spend more time with them, but this desire is thwarted by a schedule that takes us to areas of the hospital that, frankly, don't seem as beneficial to our learnin' curve. I think there's a sense of loss on both sides that could lead to idiopathic symptoms in the children."

Whoa. Go, Summer. Zoey's stunned.

"Your point?" Pace repeats.

Summer smiles coolly. "I'll be brief. I think that it would be a therapeutic experience for the peds patients who can make the trip to join those SCRUBS who'd care to participate on an outing to the Fable Harbor Amusement Park."

Before The Virus can respond in those dulcet south-of-zero tones, Summer looks to us and continues. "So, who of you would like to join me on this outing?"

Her cat eyes glitter at us. She's anticipating The Virus's negative reaction, silently daring us to take a stand with her against Pace. She looks at Chad. Peers at Becky. Glares at Zoey. Then her radar zooms in on me.

The prey has strolled into the ambush, and the hunter has us in the sights of her thirty-ought six.

Impressed doesn't begin to cover it. I raise my hand. I'm game. Chad's index finger goes up next. Becky's third. Zee hesitates. We good-as-dead animals look at her. She blinks. Then her hand goes up, too.

Summer turns back to The Virus. "As you can see, it's unanimous."

Dr. Pace smiles. "Miss Everly," she says, and we smell Summer navel-deep in it, "your job here is to *listen*. And *learn*. If an outing with children to the amusement park would amuse you, I suggest you consider a career as a day-camp counselor."

"But—" Summer begins.

"Is English a second language for you, Miss Everly? The answer is no."

Summer's mouth sets in an angry line. I swear that steam shoots from those delicate ears.

Pace reaches into her briefcase. "If there's nothing else, I have your two-week evaluations." She dumps five envelopes on the table. "Good day."

Just like that, she's gone.

We stare at the envelopes. A long beat. Then the grab begins. Well, the other four grab. I take my sweet time. MARCH, mine says on the outside. Inside, a memo from the spirochete (a bacteria, not a virus, yes, but when it comes to Pace, I can stretch the point) to Dr. Bradley.

And I read.

• • •

E-mail
From: stevedaman@aol.com
To: tristmarch@juno.com
Re: Stevie scale

Trist—

The best noose is that I got a new voice recognition program for my computer which makes many fewer miss takes even though it makes some. Thank the Lord for small favors. I don't know what else to thank Him for. Maybe that my latest scan says my tumor is stable. Ira called to say that a doc he knows at Memorial Sloan-Kettering reviewed the scan and agrees. What a place to be, huh? Not growing, not shrinking, just stuck in the middle where they can't get to it and I can't write, type, do jack, or surf. God saying "Ha, dude!" Pissant joke. And I ain't laughing.

So about this beauty Summer. You two get it on yet? I'm pic-touring naked bodies, tequila, and a hot night that doesn't go down till the sun comes up. I'm not getting weird man but I am living vicariously. Kiss her for me one time, man. 'Cuz you could be me.

Gimme news, bro. You can't imagine the awesome waives here that you and I are BOTH missing.

Stevie

E-mail

Fr: tristmarch@juno.com

To: stevedaman@aol.com

Re: Stevie scale

Do not set your voice recognizer software to "soft female voice" for this e-mail or I shall kill you.

Report from the med front: five days crapola surf. Every day I check the forecast for the west coast of Africa. I pray for tropical waves that could form tropical depressions and turn into storms that could lash the coast and give me some real waves. Don't know what I was thinking. I surf rings around anyone out here, but it's weenie.

Thought if I couldn't surf I could fish, so I bought a surfcasting rig. Hooked a twenty-pound striper first night out. Beginner's luck. Kissed him and chucked him back into the deep, of course.

SCRUBS got our two-week evaluations today. A note inside each envelope reminded us that we were in competition with each other for the twenty-five-thou scholarship. Pace is hoping to turn us against each other. Class act, huh? She ranked our work so far a scale of 1 to 5. 1 is in the lead. 5 is in the basement. Here's The Virus's ratings:

1. Summer the scintillating

2. me

3. Zoey the irritating

4. Becky the sunny

5. My man Chad the Ingenious

Pace has it in for Chad big-time. I thought he was going to cry when he saw his evaluation. Zee looked like someone told her she'd failed arithmetic. The girl needs to lighten up a little.

Summer seems jazzed to be in comp with me for the one-spot. The irony is, she can have it. I'm in Buddha's go-with-the-flow mode. There's a meteor shower tonight—check it out, big guy—so she and I are going to the beach to watch it. I'll be looking at those meteors, but I'll be seeing you. Promise.

The tumor stable is better than the tumor unstable. Tell Ira to pull all the strings he's got. Man, I want to surf with you so bad I can taste the Hawaii ocean.

Trist

Knock, knock on the door as I finish the e-mail. Click, and it's flying to Stevie. I go to the door. It's Summer, ready to trek. I invited Zee along on this outing, but she looked at me like I had two heads. What is up with her? Chad and Becky are taking Rick and Shane up to the roof of the hospital to watch the natural light show. Rick is a great guy, always up. Not even being an eighteen-year-old guy stuck on a peds ward with all those little kids gets him down. I'm glad he and Becky are happening. Becky of the lux curves and luscious hair. Sunshine couple. Shane is Rick's dark side. Pissed at the world that his life is on hold while he waits for an organ donor that may never come.

Come to think of it, can't say I blame him.

Summer's in a white tank-top and jeans with a slender ribbon necklace. Spectacular. She's got a basket with a blanket and glass clinking. Champagne? We stroll down to the beach—it takes ten minutes tops.

I'm thinking of Stevie all the way.

We find a spot back near the dunes and spread out. Yep, it's champagne, God knows where she got it. She cracks it open and pours, clinks her glass to mine.

"Here's to the SCRUBS ranked one and two," she says.

"Here's to all of us and not to the rank bitch who ranked us," I amend.

Summer looks amused and sips her champagne.

I lean back on my elbows. "Nice shot today with the rank bitch."

"Shot down would be more like it."

"Hey, you fought the good fight," I point out.

She laughs. "I have not yet begun to fight, Tristan."

"Look, the amusement park trip is a good idea—"

"It's a *great* idea," she insists. "Those kids are so . . . I stopped over to see Kelly before she went to sleep. Her doll, Rose, was in the corner with a napkin over her head. She told me Rose was in 'time out' because she wouldn't take her insulin shot."

"Kelly's a cutie."

"More than that. Don't be fooled by that kewpie-doll little face of hers. She's older than both of us. And Jerome. He gave me this origami flower he made in art therapy. Then he invited me to an X-rated movie. Then he said to let him know if anyone messed with me, because he'd get his gang to ice 'em."

I laugh. "That's one prep school kid with a rich fantasy life."

She looks at me. "That's the whole point. Fantasy is all he's got. His entire life is the hospital. These kids deserve a trip to the amusement park."

I nod in agreement. "But you can't make it happen."

"Wrong. And how borin' of you to be like everyone else," Summer drawls.

"Meaning?"

"Meanin' people have underestimated me my whole life."

"I don't think The Virus underestimated you," I tell her. "You're number one."

"I won't be for long if she hears you reelin' off med dictionaries like baseball stats. How do you do that, anyway?" She sips her champagne.

"I read a lot."

She fixes those eyes on me. "So do I, Tristan. And I'm good. No, I'm great. But I don't know half of what you know. What I want to know is, how do you know it?"

This is not somewhere I want this conversation to go. Maybe everything about me is buried in my SCRUBS file. But at least The Virus hasn't made that public. Yet. And my privacy is more important than her effing rankings.

Instead of answering I deftly change the subject. "So, how do you think you're gonna get The Virus to let you do this amusement park trip?" I ask.

She glances at her luminous watch. "Note that at eleven-fifteen I became aware that Mr. March used a diversionary tactic to avoid the question I will temporarily table."

I laugh. "You're something else."

"Glad to see you realize that," Summer drawls. "Now, would you care to make a gentleman's wager on that peds trip to the amusement park?"

I smile. "I learned a long time ago that when a lady offers you a gentleman's wager, the best policy is to run away as fast as you can."

She's all hot innocence. "Really? We wouldn't be wanting that, would we?" She pours me more champagne. My eyes flicker between the vastness of the universe and the universe that is Summer.

At this moment Summer wins. "No," I say. "We wouldn't." I kiss her softly.

She pulls away, smiles, dips her finger into her champagne, traces my mouth with it. "I'll bet that by the end of next week, Dr. Pace will approve my trip."

"I'm not betting against you."

"Good. Because you'd lose." She lies down on her back, gazes up at the stars. "I'm not the kind of girl who takes no for an answer. Not when I really want something.''

"Is that so?"

"So," Summer replies. All our eyes on the sky. A meteor arcs across. It's dazzling.

"You make a wish?" I ask her.

She turns her head to me. "I don't believe in wishes."

"What do you believe in?"

"Happiness. Success. Being prepared."

I feel something placed in my hand.

It's a square covered in foil.

She's prepared, all right. As am I, but I'll bow to the lady. I think of Stevie. I make a wish on that meteor for him. Then, there's the sweet breeze of Summer in my arms, the surf lapping at the shoreline, and I'm not giving Summer "no" for an answer.

The next day we have the morning off. I don't see Summer until lunch. She acts the exact same way she acted toward me yesterday. Mostly friendly. Somewhat cool. Sometimes flirtatious.

I'm clueless about how she feels. Even *if* she feels.

Which I decide is fine. We are . . . whatever we are. It's not like I'm after love in the romantic sense. I'm highly dubious that such a thing actually exists. Or maybe it does but only if you're one of the fortunate few who meet The One. Everyone else is settling, telling themselves that what they have is what they had in mind.

Versus that, I choose variety. And freedom.

After lunch Tia sends Chad and me to observe in the physical therapy complex. Chad tries to trade assignments with Becky, who's going to nuclear med. But Tia can't change the assignments. Chad's in a major-league funk over Pace's evaluation. I tell him two weeks into this, an evaluation is meaningless.

We both know that isn't true.

Physical therapy has its own little building off the main hospital. There's a gym where anyone can train, next door to that is a huge physical-therapy gym with all kinds of equipment.

I hate gyms. Hate treadmills. Running to nowhere while staring at a wall or a TV strikes me as a particularly uninteresting form of insanity. My heartbeat's 51 b.p.m. anyway, so I won't be hitting the rubber running rut.

We're heading down the connecting corridor to the PT building when a young woman and a guy, both in white med jackets, round the corner toward us.

Chad sees them, grabs my arm in a death grip, and pulls me into an open doorway.

We're standing in a supply closet.

He tells me, "Shut up and don't move."

Whoa. Is he hearing voices in his head? Schizophrenia? Multiple personality disorder? Acute paranoia, maybe?

The woman and the man walk past the room without looking in our direction. Chad wilts against the wall. He's actually sweating.

"You going to explain this?" I ask him.

He sucks air. "Her," he croaks.

"Her who?"

"Her," he says again, significantly. *"Her."*

"Either we're heading for acute care, or you gotta say more than 'her,' man."

Chad sticks his head out the door and looks both ways like he's in some really cheesy spy movie. He breathes a sigh of relief, turns to me. "What I'm about to tell you is totally private. Okay?"

I nod.

"Remember I told you about how I got interested in medicine? A girl named Eve?"

"Yeah. You had a big crush on her." I'm thinking what does this have to do with the price of oil in Prudhoe Bay?

"That was her."

Interest piqued now. "What, who, that woman who just walked down the hall?"

"Yeah," he confirms.

"Yeah?"

"Yeah."

We're into yeah mode now. I decide to go for a little male-bonding. "So, cool. Go up to her and tell her how much she inspired you, and wow, what a coincidence you're both working at the same hospital. She'll feel great."

"Except it's no coincidence." He's sagging against the wall again, looking mighty grim.

"No?"

"No."

"No," I echo. Now we're into no mode. "Meaning you knew she was here?"

He nods.

"And that's why you applied for SCRUBS?"

He nods again.

"And you haven't even told her?"

Shakes his head no.

"Is this supposed to be making sense to me?" I ask.

"There's a ... complication," Chad says. "I'm still in love with her."

The look on Chad's face says that for him, Eve is The One. Truth or consequences, who knows? I've never been in any kind of love, so I can't really relate. Still, I can see my friend is hurting.

"So listen," I begin, "how about if you write her a—"

I'm interrupted by the hospital intercom system. The voice is as calm as the directory assistance operator, but the message is dire.

They're calling a code up in peds. Codes mean someone is hitting the checkout line, knocking on heaven's door, shaking hands with the Grim Reaper. Every doctor on the code team gets his or her ass to the code room asap, to try to save the unlucky someone.

What flies into my head is Rule #1 when a code is called, according to the best medical novel ever written, *The House of God*: take your own pulse.

"Code Blue, Code Blue, 5E221. 5E221. 5E221."

My 51 b.p.m. spikes. Because I decoded their code the second day I was here.

"Jesus," Chad says, good Catholic that he is.

First digit, floor. In this case, fifth, for pediatrics. Second letter, east wing or west wing. In this case, east. Next three numbers, room number. In this case, room 221.

I'm already dashing down the hall, gotta find Becky.

The code is being called for Rick and Shane's room.

8

ZOEY

Arrhythmias. Irregularities in heart rate or rhythm.

Tachycardia. Rapid heart rate. Heart beats irregularly, blood pumped inefficiently. Result? Chest pain, breathlessness, light-headedness.

Cardiac arrest. Electrical impulses to said heart are absent or disorganized. Failure to stimulate contraction of the heart muscle.

Death occurs in minutes.

In adolescents with Rick and Shane's condition, all the above are improbable.

Since Rick's now arresting, probability is irrelevant.

Ironic. Two days ago The Virus distributed ten-page handout on heart abnormalities in adolescence. Alleged purpose: prep for observation of open-heart surgery on patient, 14, with congenital aortic valve disease. Actual purpose: pop quiz orals yesterday before Dr. Bailey.

Short-term goal: proof we're the morons she knows us to be.

Long-term goal: SCRUBS' demise.

Pop quiz queries, all barked aloud: Define asymmetric septal hyperthrophy. List symptoms of bicuspid aortic valve. We'd studied. Knew answers. Bailey beamed. Pace paced. Bailey left.

Then Virus spontaneously combusted.

Ultimate goal: thwarted. Temporarily.

We're outside Rick's room. Inside, Dr. Vic and crash team shock him back to life. Alive. Then dead. Then alive again.

Lots of kids with us. Kelly in my arms. Jerome announces he's an old hand at cardiac arrests, it's no biggie, man. Angela Cowen, college kid with brain-tumor symptoms not yet diagnosed, slams shut her door.

Can you blame her?

Shane's losing it. He's as dark as Rick is sunny. Twins identical only on the outside. What's he thinking? "Why Rick?" "Thank God it's Rick!"

Both?

Becky and Chad comfort him and he isn't comforted, Becky gray under golden skin and praying in Hebrew. Summer holds a girl with leukemia. Tristan with Amie, a.k.a. Junior Gwyneth.

Kelly to me: "Can God make mistakes?"

Oh, yeah, I wanna say. I don't.

Me to Kelly: "Don't know."

Chad overhears, reaches over to smooth Kelly's hair: "I don't think God makes mistakes, sweetie. It's just impossible for us to understand why God does what He does."

How Hallmark Card. I'm not buying, and if Kelly does, she isn't saying. She climbs down, goes to Summer, but there's no room, so she leans in, thumb in mouth.

I feel like Schlitz. What good is "I don't know"?

I go to Becky, rub her back. She opens her eyes.

"The funny thing," she says, smile tremulous, "is I don't believe you can petition God with prayer."

"Cover all bases just in case."

She nods. "Want to hear something crazy? I have a boyfriend in New York. His name is Malcolm. He's great, really. We've been going out for more than a year. But all I care about is Rick."

I think: Rick is on the brink of death and incredibly needy. Florence Nightingale kinda complex. Saving sick guy feels more to you like love than love.

But maybe I'm a cynical bitch and Rick is The One. If there is such a thing. Doubt has been my middle name for four long years.

Becky takes my hand. "He has to live. I didn't even get to tell him that I love him yet."

Shane stares hard at the door. "Sometimes I wish he'd just die," he bleats.

Becky blanches.

"What, you think being alive like this is worth it?"

"Yes," she says.

A dark laugh as he stomps away.

An eternity. Finally the door opens. Dr. Vic.

Shane goes to her. Like, well?

"He's stable," Dr. Vic says.

He doesn't blink. Simply turns and goes to his wheelchair. Becky throws arms around Dr. Vic, who hugs her back.

"I knew my man would make it," Jerome blusters, doing hand-slap thing with Chad. "Mah man Rick is tough-enuf!"

Kelly to Dr. Vic: "Did you make Rick all better?"

"He's still sick, honey," Dr. Vic says.

"I thought you were making him better."

"We're working on it."

Kelly nods. "It's very sad."

"Can I see him?" Becky asks.

"No. He's sedated. Maybe later." Dr. Vic's eyes stay on Becky a beat too long. Oblivious Becky.

I'm thinking Dr. Vic's thinking: why is this SCRUB so interested (Read: overly involved) with this patient?

And I'm thinking Dr. Vic's thinking: this is not at all good.

Hours later, standing outside Angela's room, listening to Dr. Vic. Rick now off ventilator. Becky got to hold his hand and talk to him.

She comes out of his room and hugs me. "You know what's really stupid? If you care about someone and don't tell them."

"You told him?"

She nods. Radiant. Her happiness lights up the peds floor. We're all happy, too. For Rick, for her.

But if Rick had died, life and medicine would march on. We'd still be standing. A lesson I learned only too well.

"Miss Cowen's CAT scan reveals no mass, no sign of a growth," Dr. Vic reports. "She does, however, have generalized cerebral swelling. Pseudotumor."

The Virus has been hovering, drifts over to listen in. Most unusual.

"And a pseudotumor is—?" Dr. Vic asks.

"Signs of a growth without its actual presence," Chad pipes up.

"Excellent," Dr. Vic says.

Chad beams, finally nailing one in front of The Virus.

"Next diagnostic step, Mr. Rourke?"

Chad blanches. Pace grins.

"Spinal tap?" Chad finally ventures.

"Correct again, Mr. Rourke."

Chad glows. The Virus glowers. Then she marches off. Who knows why she showed in the first place.

Tia and Michelle roll over a tray with spinal tap supplies as Macho-Man Mario—Mach, everyone calls him—walks by. Winks at Tia. ITALIAN STALLION's tattooed on his bicep. Always wears sleeves rolled so said self-mutilation can shine.

Tia actually blushes.

"Follow me, please," Dr. Vic orders.

We tromp in to observe spinal tap. Angela looks

ready to levitate from fear. Dr. Vic tries to calm her and fails, turns her into fetal position and swabs spine with alcohol.

Between third and fourth lumbar vertebrae, I'm thinking. Soon the needle will puncture Angela's tender flesh, exactly there.

A tear slides down Angela's cheek. She knows the truth: tap = excruciating. Even life-threatening. Catastrophic drop in spinal-fluid pressure. Brain drain. Human goes in, walking veggie rolls out.

Nurse injects lidocaine to numb pain. Ha. Dr. Vic lifts long 22-gauge needle.

A sudden beep. Everyone jumps.

My pager and Tristan's.

"You must always turn those off if you are observing a delicate procedure," Dr. Vic says sharply.

I nod too many times. Double, triple sorry. Beeper reads: ER. We both back out of the room.

Dr. Bailey paging us. Why us two? No one says.

It turns out that Fable Harbor Heli Tours does big biz giving helicopter rides to tourists. Big fun.

Unless your helicopter happens to crash.

One is down in the ocean. Five people picked up by the Coast Guard. Four alive, one more dead than alive.

Ambulances arrive. Organized chaos.

Room 1: Female, early sixties, blond hair plastered to scalp reveals gray roots. She's shivering, dazed, manic.

"I heard a pop and I asked my grandson, did you hear that, and then we landed in the water. It was gentle, not like a crash, really. Not like in the movies. The pilot opened the door. We didn't go all the way under the water. I just undid my seat belt and got out. I looked around for Kevin. He's my grandson. He's starting high school in the fall. He's so excited. He wants to be on the tennis team. Someone said he couldn't get his seat belt undone. I tried to go back for him. I thought he was already out, you see. I never would have left him. Never. He's so young and strong. He's fourteen!''

A nurse gives her a shot (Read: serious sedation). We go back to the hallway, overhear snatches of conversation.

"Seat belt got stuck."

"Coast Guard couldn't get to the kid—''

"Oxygen-deprived for how long? Bad news, man.''

"Water temp was pretty low that far out, so maybe—''

I fill in: maybe he'll live. And maybe he's about to check out at the ripe old age of fourteen.

We're now in Trauma Slot 1, out of everyone's way. Kevin. Age fourteen. Or maybe the former Kevin. Deathly pale. Surrounded by ER crash team. Intubated. IV lines. Zero respiration. Zero pulse.

Dr. Agonetti examines maybe-former-Kevin's eyes with ophthalmoscope. "Pupils dilated and fixed,'' he barks.

My not-dilated, not-fixed eyes slide over to Tristan. Inscrutable.

CPR. The Thumper, it's called. Rhythmically

pressing on Kevin's skinny chest, over and over. No heartbeat. No breathing.

"Breathe," I whisper fiercely. *"Breathe!"*

Flat line. But the ER team does not quit.

Tristan: nothing. He is feelings-free.

Experience self-loathing for being so attracted to him. He and Summer deserve eternity together.

"Cold water can slow down the effects of oxygen deprivation," Tristan says, his voice flat.

"I know that."

Tristan fixes on the IV lines. His voice is barely audible. "Epinephrine. A solution of point nine percent saline and one hundred cubic centimeters of fifty-percent dextrose."

The voice doesn't vary. Eerie. And how does he know what would be in the IV?

A nurse loudly reports Kevin's blood readings.

"Blood oxygen thirty millimeters of mercury," Tristan goes on. Same low, weird voice. "One hundred is normative. Carbon dioxide levels double normative. Probable causation, water sitting in patient's Schneider's alveoli. Air cells in the lungs through which oxygen moves toward blood and by which carbon dioxide is withdrawn from blood capillaries. Gases cannot be expelled past blockage. Collapse of the alveoli walls. Patient goes into atelectasis, meaning imperfect extension. Suffocation. Death inevitable."

Jesus.

Robot Tristan is a walking medical diagnostic text. Crash team looks defeated. Regards Dr. Agonetti.

They wait. Dr. Agonetti nods. Abandon hope, all ye who enter here. He looks disgusted, takes it personally. Marches past us and we follow.

Kevin's grandmother stands in the hall, eyes huge. Agonetti turns back to us. "Get your chicken-ship asses back in there," he barks. He heads for Kevin's grandmother, we skulk back into Trauma 1, where two nurses clean up what used to be a fourteen-year-old boy who was so excited about starting high school. Lines cut, but left in for coroner. Body cleaned. Wrists wrapped in gauze.

They are gentle with him.

It's my mother on the table.

My father.

I don't want to see this. I have to. I want to cry. I don't. There's a death certificate to be filled out. Kevin gains a number. A slot opens up on the high school tennis team.

Back into the hall at last. Newspaper vultures mill in the waiting room. I see faces, hear voices, gotta getta story.

Surreal.

I look for Tristan. He's gone.

Leo wheels a green metal boxlike thing on a stretcher toward Trauma Room 1. For Kevin's body. He sees me.

"Trist went out there." Cocks his head toward the fire escape door. "This bites, huh?"

I nod.

"Heard it's a kid."

"Fourteen," I say.

Leo shakes his head. "Man, I can't wait to get my ass outta here and get to Hollywood."

Like fourteen-year-olds don't die in Hollywood.

Up many flights of stairs, and out on the roof. People come here to breathe. To cry. To scream.

Tristan alone, eyes on the ocean. I have followed someone I dislike. Refuse to self-analyze obvious character flaw.

"Damn thing blocks the view," he says.

Meaning the medical school. Meaning the ocean. When there's more light you can see it, a little. But dusk has turned to night.

"That sucked."

He says nothing.

"You never get used to it," I go on. "My parents were doctors. They told me that."

He doesn't ask about past tense "were." I'm glad.

Instead he murmurs: "The world makes no damn sense."

I second that motion.

"Maybe the Buddhists have it right, and the kid died for some karmic reason, and he's going on to another life to work it all out, I say."

And maybe, I think, (read: you gotta admit it's just as likely) The Virus is the reincarnation of Saint Joan of Arc.

Tristan wipes his hand over his face. "What the hell am I doing here?"

Even if it's just the hormonal call of the wild, the thought of him *not* being here hits hard.

Erin's voice: "For God's sake, just do him and get over it!"

I cryogene my libido. "What *are* you doing here?"
"Paying a debt."

I'm nosier than he is. Or less self-involved. "To
who?"

"When I was thirteen, I got snow-blinded in a dog-
team comp—I woulda won that sucker, too—still
pisses me off. Dr. Ira Lynch was my ophthalmologist.
Little, squirrelly looking guy. He was a chess fiend,
so we played every day. I beat him almost every day,
though I was playing blind. You know, in my head.

"My dad was too busy to pay any attention to
me," Tristan rolls. "Big cliché there, right? Dr.
Lynch filled in. One day I reel off all this medical
stuff to impress him. It worked. He gave me all these
tests, told me I have a photographic memory. Yeah,
so? I knew I remembered everything I read, and I read
science and medical books for fun and it didn't seem
like such a big deal. 'The tests you just took were for
third-year medical students and you aced them,' he
tells me. Whatever. What I care about is, he's paying
attention to me. When I got my sight back, he stayed
my friend. We played chess by phone once a week,
for the next five years."

"He told you about SCRUBS?"

"Submitted me blind, so to speak, the sneak. Next
thing I know Dr. Bailey is sitting in my father's
cabin."

"He's *what*?"

"They came after me like I'm the next Dr. Gallo."
Read: the guy who discovered the HIV virus.

I'm still digesting that Dr. Bailey flew to *Alaska*. To *recruit* him.

"He sells me on FHUH and SCRUBS," Tristan goes on. "Only I'm not sold. Gonna spend my summer surfing with my friends Stevie and Billie. So, thanks, but no thanks."

"Wait. You turned him *down*?"

"I was going to. But . . . I didn't."

"Why?"

"Stevie."

That's not exactly an explanation.

I wait.

"Something came up. Ira helped Stevie. I did what Ira wanted me to do. So here I am."

More unsaid than said. Typical irritating Tristan.

"You took the place of some other person who desperately wanted to be here, as a *favor*?" I hope my voice is withering. I intend withering.

Tristan the head case doesn't bother to answer.

Fine. I walk away to the other side of the roof. He's an egocentric, self-involved head case. Read: clearly not into me. So as of this minute, I'm off the lust train.

I'm heading back to him to tell him off, over and out.

He comes to me first. "I left a lot out," he admits.

"No Schlitz."

"I really hate that fake-cursing thing you do."

"Am I supposed to care?"

He sighs. Like I am just *so* annoying.

"My friend Stevie has a brain tumor. Inoperable.

And no money. Dr. Lynch—Ira—makes sure he sees the best doctors and gets the best care. Medicine is cool. It's hospitals that suck.''

Oh.

It's my turn not to look at him. He's standing kiss-ably close. I feel heat. Consider suggesting rooftop quickie. Resist. Worry about mental health.

I contemplate the F-word.

Friendship.

"I never did get that surfing lesson," I murmur, reduced to twelve-year-old who likes cutest guy in school.

"Didn't you find another teacher?"

"Didn't work out," I lie. "You still up for it? We have the day off tomorrow."

"I've got a better idea. I'm heading up to New Hampshire to do the snow on Mount Washington. You up for it?"

"You're planning on mountain-climbing? In the snow? It's almost July, if you recall."

He laughs. "Snow. Climb Tuckerman's Ravine and snowboard the headwall. It's killer. I called the park service. It's passable."

"You're kidding."

"Nope. It's extreme, though. I guess an Okie girl like you doesn't snowboard—"

"Hey, I snowboard."

"Yeah?"

I nod.

"So, you into it?"

"Sure."

He smiles slowly. "All right."

Casual. Not a date. It's the F-word.

My butt.

Here's the truth: I just saw a fourteen-year-old boy die. But that night I lay in bed full of delicious anticipation.

Life is for the living, my father used to say.

Maybe. Or maybe that's just a way to excuse our selfish, shallow selves.

I finally fall asleep, not knowing.

I dream of Tristan.

9

TRISTAN

I look down over the huge lip of the headwall atop Tuckerman's Ravine. I whistle.

Now, that's steep. Really steep.

"It's at least a six-foot dead-air drop till you contact snow," I tell Zoey, "and then you'd better connect on your first turn, or it's a helluva slide to the bottom."

She nods, cool-on-ice.

Her eyes hidden behind black-rimmed shades. Red windbreaker matches the bloom in her cheeks from the morning chill.

I bet her lips would taste like cherries.

Whoa. Where did that come from?

Back to business. I cock my head downward. "The snow stops way down there," I point out. "Rocks start. Sliding in on your back would not be a good idea—''

"Which is why I suggest you don't fall," she tells me sweetly.

Funny girl. I look left. A line of skiers and boarders in the early-morning sunshine mulls the same scene. None of them looks ready to make his move. They were a lot more courageous on the way up the hill, doubtless. Zoey's looking, too. Shading her eyes from the morning sun.

"You sure you're okay?" I ask. "This is the toughest run in the East."

She smiles smugly. "You know KT-Twenty-two?"

"Squaw Valley—1960 Winter Olympics," I say. "Steepest of the steep."

She nods. "I own it."

Now, I've skied KT-Twenty-two. I'm a double black diamond skier and boarder and no way do I own it. And if there's one thing I can't stand, it's bravado. Just who does she think she's bull-shifting? As she would say.

"O'TWIT," I comment.

"The last name of an Irish friend?" she ventures.

"Only Time Will Tell," I translate.

She doesn't bother to respond. Which is so annoyingly Zee. Though I have to admit, she's hung mighty tough so far. Maybe she'll hang tough now.

Roll the tape to "start." We borrow Leo's car, leave Fable Harbor at midnight. Talk about rock 'n' roll, books, movies, sing along to the oldies station, three-and-a-half-hour drive to Pinkham Notch. Rent boards, boots, etc., at the all-night ski shop that caters to Tuckerman's idiots like us.

The sun isn't up yet, mind you. It's June. And we're going snowboarding.

She's totally into it like a little kid on her birthday or something. As out of her mind as I am.

We get to the mountain and up there is Tuckerman's. The legend. A huge bowl carved into the side of Mount Washington, biggest in New England, home of the strongest wind gust recorded in the history of history, magnet for brutal weather and huge snow dumps.

People have been skiing here late in the season forever. July fourth, even. This was a huge snow year, and there's still skiable terrain on the headwall, though every ski area with lifts has been closed since late April.

The going gets tougher as the late season goes on, too. Less snow, more rivers of snowmelt running through it. Nasty boulders that want to eat you for breakfast.

And you have to hike in, you understand. No chair-lifts, no gondola, no tram. Your feet. Your board. Your lungs sucking wind if you're not in shape.

We cheat and catch a ride with some folks taking the auto road to the top. THIS CAR CLIMBED MOUNT WASHINGTON and all that—a German couple who snap photos all the way up. Saves us hours. Not to mention blisters.

But Zee-girl was ready, set, go to hike it. Not a

mumble not a complaint not a whine not a whisper. So far she's one hundred percent WYSIWYG, as Billie says. What You See Is What You Get.

Which means maybe the girl can really snowboard.

You brought her here, butthole, a voice says to me. *People die here. You wanna be responsible for* someone else *dying? After what you did?*

Shut up, I instruct voice. He retreats. For now.

We hike to the headwall. Skiers lined up. I can feel their adrenaline. The rush hits me. Anticipation.

Zoey's staring.

"What?" I ask her.

"Nothing."

"You know corn snow?" I ask.

"Corn snow?" she echoes.

"Slush on a slope freezes at night and melts during the day, freezes and melts, freezes and melts. It's the consistency of kernel corn," I explain.

She nods. "Corn snow."

"With corn you want to wait until it melts enough to break up, but not till it's a soupy mess that sucks at your board. Kind of killer to turn and stop. And when you're doing Tuckerman's forty-five-degree pitch, you definitely want to be able to turn and stop."

"I'll keep that in mind," she says.

Then—I swear, with no warning—she's gone.

Woo-woo! Zee launches herself over the lip. Everyone whoops. She flies through the air and slams into the snow on her edge. Bam! She brakes, rips off a jump turn. Bam! Another. Bam! Another. Bam! Another.

I'm high watching her. Crazy high, every part of me feels alive, revved, on fire.

So I launch myself, too, to the whoop chorale.

Gut-checking drop, downhill edge into the snow. Lean out, I tell myself, fighting the siren song that whispers in my ear: lean in against the headwall. I give in to the song for the briefest instant and then get control of my brain. Lean in, your edge lets go. And so do you.

Bam! A turn. Bam! Another turn. Bam! Another. Then the pitch flattens from the wall of your room to the merely insane and I'm twenty yards behind Zee. We're carving figure-eights in the corn, and it's better than sex.

Almost.

More turns, more perfect corn snow, and Zee slams to a stop. I pull up next to her.

"Decent." She smiles.

Damn. Billie is the most fearless girl I know, and this run would've rocked her, I think. But not Zoey. Yet when it comes to medicine, Zee-girl gets rocked at FHUH on a regular basis.

Curiouser and curiouser.

"Want to hike up and do it again?" Zee asks me.

Before I can answer, she's gone again, carving turns like she grew up on this mountain.

I pull up alongside her. "Where'd you learn to do this?" I shout.

Her answer is to rip it downhill. I have no choice. I follow. We boogie down to where there's as much rock as snow.

Zee jams in her edge, and corn flies. I do the same. It's over. Awesome. My heart is still pounding. I'm already looking up the mountain. Already ready to do it again.

"That's when you feel most alive," she tells me.

I look at her. I'm wondering which one of us she's talking about. But I don't ask. "Where'd you learn?"

"Oklahoma."

"Bull."

"Alaska."

"Yeah. I thought I recognized you from the gondola."

She steps herself out of her bindings. I do the same. "Tell you what," she says. "We have to hike down to Pinkham Notch. So let's trade. A fact for a fact. You tell a Tristan Truth, I'll tell my snow saga. Deal?"

She's standing there in the corn snow in her boots, morning sun glinting off her hair, cherry cheeks, berry lips.

"Deal," I say. "I learned in Alaska. Mount Aleyska."

"I learned in Colorado. Vail. Two trips a year. Next?"

"Next?"

"Next," she repeats. "The Virus might have me ranked third, but I already got the Alaska thing. You owe me a Tristan Truth. Which would be something I don't know. And wouldn't even guess."

"Who made up these rules?"

"Me, of course."

She's waiting.

"Okay. A Tristan Truth. Remember when I said you have decent breasts?"

Girl Saves Man Who Isn't Drowning. She remembers. Her cherry cheeks go overripe. She nods.

"I lied. They're not decent. They're perfect."

Her face says she can't decide how to respond. Like no guy has described the beauty of her body to her before. No guy, or no guy who mattered?

Why am I wondering? Why do I care?

"And now a Zee-girl Truth," I insist.

"Zee-girl?"

I shrug. "It suits you. You said your parents *were* doctors."

A shadow clouds her face. "And here I thought you were too self-absorbed to note my use of past tense," she says.

I shake my head no.

"They're dead," she says. Then she turns her face up to the sun, closes her eyes. "They would have loved it here. Of course, they also would have kicked your ass for bringing me here."

"Nah," I say. "They would have seen how happy it made you. They would have laughed."

Her eyes pop open.

She's looking at me like: how do you know that?

I look back at her like: I don't know, I just do.

She picks up her board, slings it over her shoulder, and starts running down the trail to Pinkham Notch. And she's laughing.

I run after her, laughing, too. It echoes back up off

the headwall where we both just dodged The End.

Awesome.

We slap black flies all the way back down to Pinkham Notch. The sun blazes and I can't believe we were snowboarding—boarding!—not so long before. When we get to Leo's car, we pull out the cooler and chow down. Zee out-eats me, easy. She's utterly unself-conscious about it, too.

"Drive all night, get in one run, hike out, and drive home," Zoey says. "Totally worth it."

"Never a doubt."

She shrugs. "Most of the world would doubt it."

"To hell with most of the world," I say.

"Amen," Zee agrees, with intense fervor. She turns toward the trail that leads to the mountain. "Fluck you!" she yells at the top of her lungs.

Then this happens. I pick Zee up, as easily as if she's a kid in peds, and swing her around and around and around as we both laugh.

And then I kiss her.

A friendly kiss, I swear it. I *swear* it.

I swear it.

Zee sleeps in the car on the way back. We get into the dorm, stand in front of our doors, not wanting it to end. At least that's how I feel.

No. How we both feel. I *feel* what she feels.

"I had the greatest time," she tells me, leaning against her door.

Then she disappears into her suite. And I'm still standing there grinning like an idiot.

I turn to my door. There's a note from Chad saying he and Becky went to the movies. Cool. I could stand some time alone.

I unlock the door. The room is dark. I drop my backpack, sigh, stretch, scratch.

"Hey," a voice purrs. Definitely not Chad.

Summer.

My eyes adjust to the dark. She's in my bed. The sheet is drawn up just over her breasts. She sits up and lets the sheet fall. Clothes-free zone. She's glowing. Correction. A candle next to her is glowing. She reflects the glory.

"Your roommate's at the movies," Summer tells me.

"How'd you get in?"

"Now, is that any way to greet me?" She pouts. "How was your little outing?"

"Fine," I tell her. "Fun, actually."

"I like athletic men," she reports. Stretches her slender arms over her head.

Tired as I am, the Earth moves.

But even so, I wish she wasn't here.

"What are you waiting for?" she asks me. "You've been skiing. The shower is that way."

I know exactly where the shower is. But Summer wants to show me herself. She gets up out of bed, leads me by the hand, unbuttoning my shirt as we walk. Kissing my chest. Unzipping my jeans.

But still. From a friendly kiss with the Zee girl to this feels all wrong.

"Summer, I . . ."

"Shhhh."

She backs me into the shower. Then gets in with me.

Another guy might have been able to say no. But I think of Stevie. I remind myself that Zoey really is just a bud. And sex with Summer Everly is as close to the siren song as you can get without actually dying.

And I'm not another guy.

10

ZOEY

"Zoey." His voice is husky with passion.

Tristan's lips. On the pulse in my neck. Kiss to the beat. Oh, God. He turns me around. Lifts my hair. Hot breath. Kiss the back of my neck. How did he know to do that? A sigh. Mine. His arms around me, turning me to him. Body to body. I feel all of him. On fire. His hands. Cupping my—

"Wait. Is there a fire?" I ask.

He looks amused.

"No, I mean it. A fire alarm went off."

He pulls me to him.

I resist. "What if there's a fire?"

Smiling. "Then, you . . . stoke it."

I fall onto the bed. He stokes it. Me. Whoa. It's

everything I ever thought it would be. And more. Damn fire alarm. It won't quit and—

My eyes pop open. No fire alarm. Phone. Ringing phone. I squint at clock. It's seven in the morning. Reach for phone. Miss. Reach again. I hate whoever is at the other end, perp of *dreamus interruptus*.

"'Lo?" I croak. Eyes close.

"Is that anyway to greet a transatlantic call from your Okie sister?"

Eyes open. "Erin?"

"No, Brad Pitt After Sex Change."

I sit up. *"Erin!"*

"They do a lobotomy on you by mistake? Say something intelligent so I know it's really you," she demands.

"Getting Cafe au Laid?"

Erin's singular Erin laugh echoes through the phone.

"Now, that's better. And the answer is, does a bear schlitz in the woods? Does the Skank have permanent PMS? Am I, even as we speak, lolling on a bearskin rug, in a chalet in the Swiss Alps, clad in zip but French perfume and a dirty smile?"

"I thought you were in France with—I forget."

"Cristof, and he is so history. I met Mario two days on Boulevard St. Michel. I was trolling for postcards. He bought all the roses at the flower stand and put them into my arms as a tribute to my beauty."

"Did you have clothes on at the time?"

"Ha. He's Italian. Filthy rich. His chauffeur drove us here last night for a little vacation away from it all. It's late afternoon now, and might I add that I haven't been to sleep? Fill in the blanks and say 'Latin lover' over and over . . . and over.''

"Okie sister, how much are you embellishing for effect?''

"Your problem is, Zoey, your soul is devoid of romance. Also devoid of hot sex.''

"My soul needs hot sex?''

"*All* of you needs hot sex. Sooner the better, use it or lose it!''

"Really?'' I'm laughing.

"Ha,'' she barks. "You need to rope and cuff that guy you're always bitchin' about—''

"Rope and cuff?'' I interrupt.

"Okie flashback. I hear it happens forever after livin' there. What's that dude's name again?''

"Tristan. We've moved from intense dislike to wary friendship.''

"Bull. There was dried drool on your last letter.''

A small smile fits itself to my lips. "We spent yesterday together.''

"I need details.''

"He kissed me.'' Saying it gives body recall.

Yum.

"I knew it,'' Erin crows into the phone. "Then what?''

"Then nothing. It wasn't a *kiss* kiss.''

"My ass!''

I laugh. "That's not where he kissed me.''

"Buy some sleazy lingerie and jump him already.''

"You call from the Alps to tell me to jump him?"

"Someone has to run your pathetic excuse for a life. At least admit that you want this guy."

I struggle. "Maybe."

"My ass again. I hear the wild call of the boo-tay."

"He's involved with someone else."

"Mario is married, what's your point?"

"Erin!"

"Who are you, the morals squad? I'm just playing. This isn't real life."

"His wife might disagree."

"Jump out my ass, Zoey."

Time to change the subject. "How's your shoulder?"

"Mario licks the scar."

I wince. "More than I needed to know."

"So's this, but it's so kinky you're gonna love it, anyway. Last night we— Whoops, guess who just walked in. *Buon giorno*, Mario!" she calls.

A male voice. Italian-accented English, and he sounds pissed.

"Zoe? Gotta run."

I get a funny feeling. "You sure you're safe?"

"Please, he's harmless."

"I'm serious, Erin. Give me a number where—"

"Ciao!" She hangs up just as the door opens.

Becky enters, the Curvy Good Witch Of The North, all sunshine and happiness. Carrying wildflowers, obviously just picked. " 'Morning. It's so amazing out!'' She gets a water glass, fills it, arranges flowers. Hums.

"Way too sunny on way too little sleep," I tell her, squinting. "I need shades to look at you."

"You need to jump in the shower and come have breakfast with me before we face Dr. Davis." She glances at her watch. "In exactly forty-five."

I throw the covers back, stand up, stretch. "I showered when I got in last night." I pad to the bathroom to do a.m. bathroom thing. "You were still out. So was Scarlett."

Becky's face appears in the bathroom doorway. Eyes shining. "I spent the night with Rick."

I choke on Colgate. "Spent the night? Or *spent the night?*"

Curvy Good Witch, against the wall, in bliss: "You know Rick and Tia are friends, right?"

"Tia's friends with everyone." I spit, exit bathroom, pull jeans and a T-shirt out of a drawer. Have to switch to dreadful redfuls when I get to the hospital, anyway.

"But they're *really* good friends," Becky explains. "So, last night, we're hanging out in his room. Shane wheels in—I don't know where he was—but anyway, he says 'I want to crash,' meaning time for me to get my butt outta there, right? So Rick says he has a surprise for me. We go to that wing on four that hasn't been renovated yet. And he unlocks a door. To a little room where the on-call doctors used to crash before they built the new rooms on five. And this little room has a little bed in it."

"You're kidding," I say. "Tia gave Rick a key?"
Becky nods.

"He wasn't hooked up to his heart monitor?"
She shakes her head.

"Weren't you worried about his heart?"

"We just macked and all that. Mostly we held each
other and talked. The first time we make love is not
going to be at Effing-Huh."

I think: if an organ donor doesn't come, you could
be waiting a really long time. And: she's picked up
my pet name for the hospital.

But I can't focus on that now.

"So, like, all night?" I ask.

She nods. "And we still have the key."

I smile. Read: cover up incredulity. "Look, I know
you're happy. And I'm happy for you. But if you got
caught, The Virus would kick your butt outta here so
fast—"

"We're not gonna get caught."

"But if you do? Pace could blackball you from
ever getting into med school—"

"I thought you'd be happy for me!"

"I am, but—"

She holds a hand up to me, palm out. Read: shut
up.

"Have you ever been in love?" she asks me.
Tristan. His kiss . . .
"No."

Becky smiles. "Then you don't know. Ready to
go?"

I grab my father's former medical bag, and we truck over to the hospital.

"Summer must have gotten in really late," I say. "And gotten up really early." Read: me, fishing for info. I know she wasn't with Tristan. *I* was with Tristan.

But it pays to keep tabs on the enemy.

"I think she hung out on four last night," Becky reports. "It's weird, huh? How she's so great with the peds kids and such a bitch with everyone else?"

"It's a Triple B thing," I say. "So everyone can say how marvelous she is to suffer the little children, bless her heart. I don't know what Tristan sees in her, beyond the obvious."

Eyes slide to Becky. Read: me, fishing again.

She twists a Scrunchie in her hair. "You so sure they're a thing?"

As we enter the already-crowded cafeteria, get trays, get in line: "Aren't you?"

Becky shrugs. "She flirts with him. But Scarlett flirts with everything that zips at the crotch."

"So you don't think they're a thing?"

Becky's face goes wise. "I'm so on to you."

I redden, fill a coffee mug. "What?"

"Just what happened with you two yesterday, anyway?"

"Nothing. We had fun." Cereal, yogurt, two huge muffins hit my tray while I try to act casual.

We play bumper people, dodge through the crowd, stake out a table. Becky sips her juice, regards me. "More or less fun than I had last night?" she asks.

"It's not like that."

"Uh-huh." Tiny knowing smile.

"Okay, I might like him," I admit. "A little."

Said smile does not dissolve.

"Okay, more than a little."

I'm breakfasting across from Mona Lisa.

"Look, we're just friends," I explain. "Which is better than when we hated each other's guts, right? And nothing happened yesterday. I mean, we talked. And laughed. And went snowboarding. Don't ask where. Okay, he kissed me. But it wasn't a *kiss* kiss. I don't think. Do you think it could have been? No, it wasn't."

Belly laugh from Becky. "Get a load of you!"

"So happy I amuse you."

"You'd better rethink your answer to that question I asked you this morning."

"What?" I ask.

She doesn't answer. Doesn't have to. She knows I know. And I know she knows I know.

Have you ever been in love?

11
ZOEY

"Yo, it's the Grateful Reds," Marcus the orderly jokes as he bops by us red-clad SCRUBS. We await Dr. Davis in front of the pediatric nurses' station.

Nurse Michelle is out sick. Floater nurse Hirsute Harriet (read: mustachioed by-product of hormonal confusion) gives a baritone snicker. Lark, red-haired nurse with protozoa brain, doesn't get the joke.

Marcus spies Tia at elevator. Hurries over. She seems glad to see him, goes all girly. No accounting. My eyes slide to Tristan, deep in conversation with Chad. If I go all girly around him, shoot me and put me out of my misery.

He and Summer showed up together this morning. I go all weird. Tell myself it didn't mean jack. Try to pick up their vibes for each other. Fail. Try to suss out Tristan's vibes for me, post yesterday. Fail again.

Elevator spews out Dr. Bailey. His face belongs on Mount Rushmore. Could play himself in a movie.

"Good morning," he says, beaming at us.

We murmur appropriately.

"So, how's it going for you young people?"

More sycophantic murmurs.

"Wonderful." He nods. "Dr. Pace tells me you're all making significant progress. Most exciting. I've been encouraging her to write a paper on SCRUBS for one of the major journals."

Can't wait to read it.

"Please feel that my door is open if I can be of any help to you young people," Dr. Bailey adds. Turns to Summer. "Ms. Everly, if I might have a word with you?"

"Certainly, Dr. Bailey," she replies. Like he chats her up every day. Like they're colleagues. Unreal.

They walk off. Tentacles of insecurity grab my throat. Dr. Bailey has never asked if he could have a word with *me*.

The Virus ranks Summer number one. Summer is: gorgeous, rich, smart, utterly self-assured. Summer has: showed up with Tristan. Summer is: having "a word" with Dr. B.

I am: none of the above.

I think of Erin, watching Triple P Delia Lamont get down at Cafe au Laid.

I can take her.

Dr. Davis and his scowl exit Kelly's room. Six

med students in white jackets trail behind. Davis heads for us. Scans the Scrubs Red Sea.

"Someone is missing."

"Ms. Everly is with Dr. Bailey," Chad volunteers.

On Davis's disdain: "Did I *ask* you, Mr. Rourke?"

"No, sir."

"When I *ask*, please feel free to volunteer information. If you ever have any that is useful, that is."

Chad shrinks. Med students preen.

Davis turns to Hirsute. "The chart on Four C?"

Becky and I trade looks. Room 4C is Angela the pseudotumor. Last seen mid spinal tap. Before Tristan and I got beeped to ER to watch a fourteen-year-old die.

Hirsute finds chart. Makes hairy handoff. Davis scans chart while we wait. I wish we were with Dr. Vic. Davis gets off on humiliation. Calls patients by their room number. Wants SCRUBS going, going, gone.

"Room four is a nineteen-year-old Caucasian female who presented with double vision, headaches . . ." Davis drones.

On-and-on Anon in action. Tells what we already know. None of us has the nerve to tell him. We stand there.

"Results of the spinal tap," Davis says, breaking new ground. "Four C's spinal pressure reading was many times base normal. Indicating—?"

Floor studying in action.

Davis eyes Chad. "I'm in the mood for a little light

entertainment, Mr. Rourke. Indicating what?"

Chad looks up and clears his throat. "Indicating an obstruction to the flow of cerebro-spinal fluid, sir. Such as a growth—"

Med students smug in action. Davis opens his mouth to nail Chad with no-growth news.

"Only in Miss Cowen's case," Chad continues, "no growth was apparent on her CAT scan. Which suggests a pseudotumor. Which would be in accord with Ms. Cowen's symptoms, as well as with the increase in spinal fluid pressure. Pseudotumors can be caused by obesity, diabetes, and certain medications, such as oral contraceptives. Sir."

Slack-jaw Davis. "Good, Mr Rourke—"

Yes! It is all I can do not to high-five Chi-town Chad. SCRUBS grin at him like idiots.

"—Except that Four C is not obese, not a diabetic, and does not take oral contraceptives," Bruce Frank, Future Middling MD Living In The Suburbs points out. No way pissant Chad is gonna best him *again*.

"Correct," Davis agrees. "We have here a medical mystery. Always entertaining."

"And here I thought we had a teen girl *suffering*," Becky whispers to me. Daring.

"We will now—" Davis begins, but he's beeped away somewhere. We are to await his return. Duh.

Temporary reprieve. We breathe from diaphragm again. Real med students instantly separate themselves from us.

"Excellent just now with Davis," Tristan tells Chad.

"I wish Pace had been here," Chad says. Clearly thinking about his schlitzy evaluation.

"Yo, homies, 'zup?" Jerome limps over to us on his crutches.

" 'Zup?" little Kelly echoes, walking beside him, mimicking his cool-dude bob and limp. Both wear new shades. Jerome's shorts so baggy they hang lower than leg that no longer exists.

"Not much," Chad replies, doing a hand-slide thing with Jerome. Kelly puts her hand out for one, too.

"Nice shades," Becky tells them.

"My posse came by yesterday, brought me a whole bunch of 'em," Jerome explains.

Kelly gazes at him in adoration. "They're my posse, too, right?"

"You got it, pretty momma," Jerome assures her. "You know what they told me about you?"

Kelly gazes up at her hero. "What?"

"They said you was a twenty-first-century fox."

Kelly looks confused.

"That means you fine as wine by natural design," Jerome translates.

Kelly giggles. She lost a front tooth overnight.

"Hey, y'all," Summer calls, heading for us from the elevator. Radiant.

Slide eyes to Tristan to gauge reaction. Zero.

Hirsute lumbers by with meds tray, catches sight of Summer. Sighs with longing. Mustache grows another inch.

"You're looking hot today," Jerome tells Summer, kissing her hand.

"Why, thank you, Jerome." Summer all Triple B southern charm. She reaches for Kelly, who cuddles into her arms. "I have fantastic news. On Monday we're gonna be takin' y'all to Fable Harbor Amusement Park."

"For real?" Jerome asks hopefully.

"For real!" Summer assures him. "I just got the okay from Dr. Bradley."

Joyful reaction in the under-ten set. Summer's eyes meet Tristan's. He licks a finger, marks the air with it. He's major impressed.

Everyone's laughing, asking how Summer did it, does The Virus know yet, when Davis returns.

Solemnity returns. We follow Davis into 4C, fill it wall-to-wall. Angela looks preshrunk. Miserable.

Davis barks questions at her, a cop with a known perp. Tell us: daily schedule. Diet. Medications. Street drugs.

Says she: I've told you a dozen times.

Tell us again.

Angela near tears. Clutches pillow like a life raft. "My first class is at nine. So I get up around seven-thirty. For breakfast I usually have cereal and coffee and my vitamins. If I take them on an empty stomach I get nauseated. I have a break between . . ."

She's going on, but my mind isn't. It's back on vitamins.

A memory: I'm ten. Cara Majors, newly crowned Miss Chaney the month before, sits in my parents' waiting room. I wonder why she isn't wearing her crown. She looks like a pile of puke. Yellow. Dried out. Serious zits. Ticks me off. *This* is Miss Chaney? No way she wins Miss Oklahoma. We shoulda picked a Miss Chaney who could *win*.

Cara goes into room. I follow. Mom's nurse shuts the door. Not quite all the way. I peek in.

"She takes a multiple every morning," Cara's mom says. "And vitamin A to clear up her skin for the pageant."

"How much? Too much is toxic," my mother says. "That's what's making her sick."

I blink back to Effing-Huh. Angela, mid-litany.

"How much vitamin A are you taking?" I blurt.

The room goes silent.

Davis looks at me like I just aerosoled anthrax.

Angela shrugs. "Eight a day, usually. For—"

"Your skin," I fill in. "I think Ms. Cowen has acute vitamin A intoxication."

Davis passes a kidney stone before our eyes. "Someone will be in to see you later," he tells Angela, then exits.

We file out behind him.

Davis turns on me. "If you ever, *ever* make a diagnosis in front of a patient again, I will see to it that your medical career ends before it begins. Is that absolutely clear? Or would kicking you out on your ear make it clearer for you?"

My entire self vibrates. "It's clear, sir."

"Now get out of my sight. And your asinine redcoated friends can join you."

The mother-flucker will not get the satisfaction of seeing me cry. I stride to fire exit, head for the roof.

And then I'm weep city.

I suck. I blew it.

Et cetera.

From behind me: "Let's string him up by the short hairs."

Tristan. My back is to him. I push away tears. "Go away."

"He's pissed 'cuz you got it right. I knew right after you said it. She's taking toxic levels of vitamin A."

Sniffing back snotty tears. "Why does someone as loathsome as Davis become a doctor? He hates people."

"Power, maybe. Listen, you were brilliant."

Bitter laughter. "I'm sure Davis will note that on my dismissal letter."

"He won't do squat."

"You don't know that."

"Think about it. He'd have to admit that you caught something he missed. No way he puts that in writing."

Maybe. Tristan pushes something into my hand. A red bandanna. I blow and wipe, blow again. Pocket snot rag. Turn to him. "Thanks. I'll wash it."

He smiles. "Like my Hawaiian shirt."

Oops. "I forgot."

"Just busting your chops. Better?"

I nod. Will him to put his arms around me. Fail.

"How did you come up with vitamin A toxicity, anyway?" he asks me.

"My mom. I miss her so much." Tears spill. It's so not me. He holds me, finally. I press against his chest. He strokes my hair. I pull myself together. Re-use snotty snot rag. Repocket.

"We're pretending this never happened," I warn him.

"What?" he asks, smiling.

Because of him, I'm able to return to the land of the living.

Because of Tristan.

That night, late. One of my roommates saws wood. Too dark to see who. I'm on a hot date with my steady: insomnia. The muse I choose over my usual nightmare.

Mom. Buried alive. Bleeding. Calling me. And I can't move, can't breathe. Can't.

Failure whispers to me. At medicine. At life.

How could I blurt out my diagnosis in front of a doctor like that? How could I yearn for Tristan to kiss it and make it all better?

So not me.

The truth. I want him with every corpuscle of my being. Every particle. Subparticle. Subatomic particle. Never felt this way before. Not remotely.

I hate it.

Sleep eludes. I'm resigned. I think: a beach walk

with my steady. Pull on sweats in dark, tiptoe out. Jog to beach.

Have you ever been in love?

Becky shines with it. But how can she know, after such a short time? What if it's lust? What if she gets hurt? What if it doesn't last? What if.

The beach. I head for the dunes. Climbing them tires me out. Turns off my mind. I hope.

Maybe Erin's right. I should jump him. Get it over with. Me to him: can I pencil you in to lose my virginity?

But I want it to be special. Romantic. Candles. Wine. Tristan. Slow and soft. Hard and wet. Hot and—

Jeez, Zoey, get a grip.

What do I want? I want . . . what my parents had.

God. I am excruciating. But that's the truth. That's what I want. Doctor and Doctor. And love, too. Happily-ever-after. It's not impossible. If my parents had it, why can't I—

A soft moan. Did I hear it, really? I stop, my Reeboks sink into sand. My breathing is hard, fast, from climbing. Loud in my ears. What else? Silence. And?

Another moan. More moans. Someone cries out. Two someones. From behind the dune. A chorus of—

I know even before I look. I look anyway.

Behind the dune. Tristan. And Summer. Making love.

Funny. The sounds of her pleasure and my pain aren't so different. But she doesn't know that. Neither does he.

Because I am already going, going, gone.

12

TRISTAN

E-mail
To: stevedaman@aol.com
Fr: tristmarch@juno.com
Subj: Attack of the heart

This'll be a quickie cuz I'm seconds away from an outing to Fable Harbor Amusement Park with a bunch of peds kids and the other SCRUBS. It's billed as morale-booster. But sometimes I feel like it's the kids who boost my morale. On a more carnal subject, the divine Summer and I have, uh, shared. Even for you, details shall remain private. Okay, I'll throw you a bone, you hound dog. She walks in beauty like the night. And then she walks away. I lucked into a woman who doesn't mix up sex and love. Like Zoey would. I can tell. Good thing we're just friends. She's amazing,

Stevie. Get this—she boards like Billie surfs. We climbed and did Tuckerman's, she was a warrior girl, take-no-prisoners. She gets into my brain at the most inopportune moments. Like when I'm with Summer. That's messed up. Unfair to Summer. Not me at all. Tell anyone and you won't need to make any more brain tumor death jokes 'cuz I'll kill you. Got an e-mail from Ira who updated me on your med sitch. Trust you not to. Bummer about needing more radiation. Wish I could take it for you. I really want you to think about doing the radiation here. And no, I won't shut up about it. Aloha to you, Billie, and the ocean. E-mail me immediately.

Tristan

We're at Fable Harbor Amusement Park. It's all sunshine and primary colors. Adrenaline-pumped kids in fantasyland. And our kids are the most pumped of all.

Tia drove the large hospital van, Hirsute helped us wheel seven mighty psyched kids out of the back. The park knew we were coming and made a special effort to see we have everything we need. What we need is to let our kids have fun without getting gawked at.

We do the merry-go-round. I'm holding April Berman, age four, a little heartbreaker who wears a pink ribbon Jerome gave her wrapped around her chemo-bald head. I tell her how pretty she looks. The kid on the next horse yells, "Are you a boy or a girl?"

April tears off the ribbon and buries her head in my arms.

We go on a water ride. A big kid nudges his buds

and jeers, "Hey, hey, lookit! That black kid over there is deformed, man! He only has one leg, check it out!"

Everyone checks it out. Dozens of eyes, staring.

Jerome shoots the big kid the finger. None of us stop him. Hell, I want to applaud. I look over at Zoey, knowing she'll feel the same. But her face is stone-cold and she's staring daggers at me. What's up with that?

"No more baby rides," Jerome says, flying along on his crutches. "Let's ride the Super Spiral Roller Coaster."

"Yeah!" Orlando Ruiz agrees. He's a handsome kid, twelve, with juvenile rheumatoid arthritis so bad he's had ten joint surgeries, about to have number eleven. Sometimes he can walk with crutches, today he's in a chair.

"They haven't finished building it yet, guys," Chad tells them.

"Oh, man," Jerome groans. "This is a baby park." He plops down on a painted bench.

Tia checks her watch. "Jerome, time for your meds."

He scowls. "Aw, man," he moans, superloud so everyone knows he's moaning. "You take 'em, woman. I'm on a meds strike as of right now. Meds strike! Meds strike! Meds strike! Meds strike!"

He looks from kid to kid, trying to get it going.

"Meds strike!" little Kelly chimes in. She'd follow him to the eve of Destruction. But other kids aren't buying. They know civil disobedience is a onewayer back to FHUH. Kelly pumping her fist, and everyone cracks up.

"Oh, Je-rom-*eee*," Matt Everson calls in a girly falsetto, imitating Tia. "Be a good little boy and take your meds! Open wide!" He's thirteen but small for his age. He has a rare kidney disorder, has to wear a bag so his urine bypasses the normal exit. He hides it under sweatshirts the size of pup tents.

Matt and Orlando start razzing Jerome. The little girls giggle, except Kelly, who goes at Orlando and punches him. Hard.

"See, she's tougher than both of you wusses put together," Jerome tells the guys as Orlando holds Kelly at arm's length.

Tia pushes Jerome's meds out to him.

"At my other hospital," Jerome says, "I used to skip my meds all the time. Tia, woman, I'm callin' my gang on my cell phone. They gonna come ice you. Right here. You ain't walkin' out of this place alive."

Tia laughs. As do we all. Jerome finally throws back the pills with a water bottle chaser.

"What you lookin' at, son?" Jerome scowls at me. "You never do Everclear?"

I hold my palms up. "Hey, I'm cool, man."

"All right, then." Jerome adjusts his shades, all bad-ass dude. Kelly does likewise and takes his hand.

Tia and Hirsute check the meds list and schedule for the whole group. Really, though, we're giving them all a chance to rest. Kelly chatters away to Zoey, who listens as if the kid has the cure for cancer. Now, that's cool.

"This is great, huh?" Summer sits next to me, raises her face to the sun.

"You still haven't told me how you pulled this off."

"I might have told Dr. Bradley that the amusement park was Pace's idea. She couldn't contradict him when he was congratulating her on her brilliance, now could she?"

"Is that what you did?"

"Or I might have flashed Dr. Bradley my G-string," she went on. "Which color-coordinated perfectly with the decor of his office."

"Did you?"

She smiles. "All that matters is that I won our bet, Tristan." She looks to Tia, who nods that rest time is over.

"Hey, ya'll, who wants to go on the Ferris wheel?" Summer asks.

Chorus of *me!*s erupts. "All right, then," she says, "line up by me."

You never saw sick kids move so fast. An instant line forms. Jerome at the front with Kelly, then Matt, then Chad with April in his arms. Orlando wheels over. And lastly, Amie, our junior Gwyneth, with Becky pushing her chair. Only Dawn, the other little girl with leukemia, stays in her wheelchair. She's too beat, she says. Zoey goes to talk with her.

"Impressive turnout," Becky notes.

"I love the Ferris wheel," Amie says shyly.

"How about Summer, Chad, Becky, and Harriet take the kids on the wheel?" Tia suggests. "You'll fit, it's a ten-seater. We're kind of tired, too, so we'll wait with Dawn.''

Tia-speak for: let's not let Dawn feel alone.

The group troupes and wheels off. Dawn whispers something to Tia, who mouths to us that Dawn has had an accident and she's taking her to the ladies' room.

Which leaves Zee and me.

I'm happy to be with her, haven't had a chance to talk with her all day. Did I imagine her deep-freeze?

"It's great that Summer pulled this off, huh?" I say.

"Great," she snaps.

Snaps. Zoey. At me. I am more than confused. "Did I miss something?"

"You?" Her voice drips sarcasm.

"Well, clearly you're pissed about something."

"I would have to care to be pissed, wouldn't I?"

That stumps me. I am wordless. So I reach out to touch her hair and say, "Really, Zoey, what's—"

She pulls away like I'm contaminated. "Let's just keep this professional from here on in."

Floored me. Clueless me. Stunned me. The mask is on, though. I say fine. She says thank you, like a bad play. And then I can't help myself. "I thought we were friends, Zee," I say, searching her face for clues.

"*Friends?*" she echoes. "You don't even know the meaning of the word." And just like that, she walks away.

Tia comes back with Dawn just as our group returns from the Ferris wheel. Zoey rejoins us as far from me as possible. We decide to walk over to Playland, where the kids can win stuffed animals at games of chance.

I step in near Becky. "Having fun?"

"Absolutely. I wish Rick could come, though."

"He's a great guy," I say. "Listen, is there anything up with Zoey I should know about?"

Becky shrugs. "Beats me. Why?"

"Nothing."

So Becky doesn't know anything about what's going on with bi-polar Zoey, either.

"Lookit!" Kelly cries, pointing to a double-decker merry-go-round that puts the kiddie one to shame.

"Aw, man," Jerome says. "I don't need to ride another pretend pony. I bet on the horses, man."

And I'm betting he's on a horse within five minutes.

I win. I lift him up on a painted unicorn on the top deck, stand by him and watch his balance. He whoops louder than anyone else.

"Yo, Orlando!" he calls. Orlando's atop a purple camel across the way.

" 'Zup, Jerome?" Orlando yells.

Jerome points to his watch. "Time for your meds, dude!"

"Aw, man!" Orlando pouts.

"Bustin' his chops," Jerome confides. Kelly's riding a hot-pink filly. He blows her a kiss.

The merry-go-round slows and stops. It takes us a while to get all the kids off. They're all screaming for ice cream from the kid in the white uniform. Hirsute pays and delivers. Kelly's sugar intake is carefully monitored. She settles for a lick of Summer's Popsicle and a sugar-free cookie from Tia's bag. She's bummed.

Tia the party-pooper calls time for rest and meds. The kids sprawl on the grass in the area between Crack-the-Whip—forget it, Jerome, you are not going on that!—and a construction zone around the half-built Super Spiral Roller Coaster. Two huge construction cranes are parked side by side behind a Cyclone fence topped with barbed wire.

"Tristan, what's it say?" Kelly asks, nibbling her cookie. She points at a sign on the barbed wire.

"It says, Kelly: you better keep out of this area or you're going to have to kiss Orlando a lot of times."

She shrieks, giggles. "Never, never, never!"

"That's 'cuz she's my lady," Jerome explains breezily.

"I thought I was your lady," Summer objects.

Jerome shrugs. "Yeah, well, you know how it is."

I laugh, and that's when it happens.

Why it happens is irrelevant.

One crane building the Super Spiral starts tipping, almost in slo-mo. It doesn't seem real. But then it's like—*wham!*—slamming into the other crane. A spaghetti of twisted metal comes crashing down.

Right at us.

Everyone screams and tries to bolt. April can't move. I leap at her and fling her away with all my might. Crane metal slams into Crack-the-Whip. More metal snaps.

Kelly! I lunge for her.

Then, blackness.

13

ZOEY

Nightmare. No, daymare. I'm awake. This is happening. Now. Really happening.

First thought: The Virus is gonna kill us.

Second thought: Are all the kids okay? Trapped?

Third thought: Not again. Please, God.

Fourth through sixth thoughts: Murrah. Dad. Mom.

Banish one, three, and four-through-six. Squelch scream. Scramble to round up all kids. Chad helps. Becky and Summer. Hirsute.

The pile of twisted metal shifts precariously. Screams from underneath it. Park personnel arrive, screaming directions that mingle with the screams from beneath the metal. There is panic. Scream city. It isn't real. But it is.

I tell myself to move. Do something. *Something*.

"Get the kids the hell out of here!" Chad is screaming.

I remember how to speak. To Summer: "Who's missing?"

"Tia, Kelly, Tristan."

I look at the twisted metal, a sculpture done by a madman. From underneath, someone cries out, high-pitched.

Kelly? Tia?

Sirens. More scream city. The cops arrive.

One demands, "What happened here?"

"The crane fell. There are people trapped under there and you have to get them out!"

"Who are you?"

"FHUH," I snap, flash my ID badge.

"Sorry, Doc," he says. And doesn't try to make me move back. Not the top of his cop class. People press in.

"Get these vultures outta here!" I yell.

He does. The power of the MD. "Move back! Move back!" he shouts, and his cohorts take up the chant.

"Where are the Jaws of Life?"

"We radioed, on their way," the cop replies. "There was a bad crash near Falmouth, though, so—" He's looking at me. Like I'm a doctor. Why aren't *I* doing anything?

So I do. Shimmy close to the wreckage on my belly.

"Hey!" I yell in. "Can anyone hear me? Help's coming!"

No answer.

"Hey!"

Weakly, back to me. "First rule: take your own pulse."

Tristan. Oh, God. Someone hands me a flashlight. I beam it in. His face. Head bleeding. Not all that far from me, though.

"The parameds are on their way," I assure him. "They'll cut you out of there. Are you okay?"

"Yeah. My leg is stuck under something, though."

"Can you see Kelly and Tia?"

"Kelly's farther back. I can just barely touch her fingers. She's doing okay, though. Pretty scared." He turns his head. "You're getting a big medal for bravery when we get out of here, Kel."

I hear her whimper. Call for momma.

"Tia?" I ask.

Tristan barely shakes his head. Doesn't want Kelly to know. Which means Tia is—

The world goes upside down. I want to faint. Can't. Hold on. "Hey, Kelly!" I yell into the rubble. "Help is coming, sweetie. If you—"

Suddenly the metal spaghetti monster lurches like it's alive. Everyone screams.

"Get back!" a cop yells.

"Mommy!" Kelly screams from underneath. "Mommy!"

A cop stands over me. "This thing could cave at any minute," he says. "You need to get back, Doc."

"Where's the rescue squad?" Summer is demanding, breaking away from the crowd.

"Ma'am, you can't—" a cop tells her.

She's not listening. She's on her hands and knees, burrowing into the metal labyrinth.

"Summer, no!"

"I'm getting Kelly out," Summer calls back.

"Summer!"

She disappears. I beam the flashlight. Reaches Tristan. Touches his cheek. Her, not me.

The It shifts again. Screams from every direction. One is mine. "Summer!"

"Here! Okay!" she yells back. "Kelly, sweetie?" she calls. "Everything's goin' to be okay. Kelly?"

"I want Zoey!" Kelly screams now. "Zoeeeeey!"

My cheek hits dirt. It's the OKC shakes. Daymare. Real this time. The world spins. I'm sorry, Momma. I can't get to you. Please don't die. Please.

"Zoeeeeey!"

You should be under there, you chicken-schlitz bitch, a voice tells me. You failed your mother. And Erin. And—

My fingernails in the ground. Force my head into the rubble. Have to do it. Can't see through my tears. In or out, which will it be?

"Out of the way, out of the way." Special rescue unit. Pushes me back. I didn't see them. Then they're snaking in and under. I'm sent back to the trenches. I go.

Becky wraps her arms around me.

First out, a body. Tia. Dead. Crushed.

Next out, in a firefighter's arms, Kelly. Alive. Barely, maybe. Her eyes meet mine. Betrayer, they say. She'd hustled into the back of an ambulance.

The rescue squad crawls out with Summer. And Tristan. They tell him to lie still, but he manages to stand up. Staggers. Passes out when they get the stretcher.

The shakes have me in their grip. Failure me. Consider throwing myself under It. Don't.

It's so much tougher to keep living.

• • •

Dear Erin,

You amaze me. I spend the whole night at the hospital while Kelly's in surgery, then out, then she bleeds internally and she's back in, then she's out and finally out of the woods, they think. I finally stagger back to unsweet suite and the phone's ringing. And it's you.

From Rome. Rome? I didn't even get how you ended up there. But it was like you knew I needed you, Okie sistuh, and I did. Don't know if I would have made it otherwise. Ten thousand thank-yous for calling, for listening to me wail. Eduardo's phone bill is going to be insane, but since you said he's even richer than Mario, maybe he won't mind. Kelly's condition has been upgraded to serious. She lost part of one kidney. Tristan's ankle isn't broken. Amazing, since something fell on it that trapped him under there. Turns out he had on some kinda schlitz-kicker metal reinforced biker boots his friend Stevie gave him. He has a concussion, though, they've still got him in the hospital because he's blacked out a couple of times.

It's over between us, anyway. Not that it ever was. He and Summer are definitely a thing. Details to come cuz I can't face 'em right now.

Tia's funeral is tomorrow. I just can't believe it. Made a condolence call to her family today, with Chad, Summer, Becky, Becky's b.f. Rick, and his twin bro, Shane. They both need heart-lung transplants. Soon. But that's another depressing story for another depressing time.

I'm mailing this to your cousin's roommate's flat in Venice, per your instructions. Nice that you've got so many European connections.

Say some prayers for I don't even know for what. I would really appreciate it if the world started making sense. If you have any pull with the higher-ups, please pass on my request. XXXXX, Okie sistuh,

Zoey

I reread my letter. Then read between the lines everything I left out. Tristan and Summer on the beach. Kelly calling for me under the rubble. Summer going to her.

And me. Not going.

"Let's call Tia's parents and send flowers to the

funeral, huh?'' Becky suggests. She's on her bed, too depressed to move.

"I already did," Summer says from her bed.

"With *all* our names?" Becky asks sharply.

"All."

Summer polishes her nails. Digging under twisted metal is hell on a manicure, I figure.

She is braver than I am. Did what I couldn't do. I should tell her. Thank her. I don't.

The clock reads nine-thirty. I jump up and push into some sandals. Tell them I'm going for a walk. Depart. Head for Tristan's hospital room. Sixth floor, W wing.

I peek in, not sure he'll be awake. Chad's with him. They're laughing. Laughing!

Chad sees me. "Hey, come on in."

I do. Tristan looks like Tristan with cuts. Read: my heart aches.

"How're you feeling?" I ask him.

"Fine. I'm outta here in the morning."

"Good." Fold arms. Shift weight. Feel like idiot.

"Sit down," Tristan finally says.

"I'm interrupting—"

"No, no," Chad says. "Trist was helping me compose a letter to—a friend from the past, I guess you could say."

"Male or female?" I ask.

"Very," Chad says. "Female," he adds.

Tristan's staring at me. Chad looks from him to me, back to him.

"Hey, I think I'll go get some dinner," he announces.

Big lie. He shared a pizza with us in our unsweet an hour ago. I don't stop him.

"So," I attempt. "You're okay?"

"I will be if you sit down."

I do. Silence. Then we both talk at once. Stop. Do it again. Stop. Laugh self-consciously. Bad scene. Cut.

"Speak," Tristan says.

Deep breath. Exhale. "I just want to say that I admire Summer for crawling in there for Kelly. And I hope the two of you are very happy together."

His face goes funny. "The two clauses of that sentence don't seem to go together."

"Fair trade," I offer. "One question each. An honest answer. A Tristan Truth for a Zoey Truth."

He nods.

"Are you in love with her?" I ask him.

Silence. Then he says, "No."

Allowing me to breathe again.

His turn. "Why do you ask?"

"I get insomnia," I say. "So sometimes at night I walk on the dunes."

He gets it.

Tristan, finally: "Why did you ask me if I love her?"

"One question per customer, those were the rules."

He nods. Folds his arms.

I stand. "So you can go to the funeral, then?"

Nod city.

"I still can't believe—"

"I know," he says.

I walk to the door, back to him. "Tristan, have you *ever* been in love?" I ask the door.

"One question per customer," Tristan reminds me.

Right. I mumble something appropriate. Flee. Jog down to the beach.

The bitch of it is, wherever I go, I'm still there.

14

TRISTAN

The sky is gray and threatening. We push into the back of the overcrowded church to witness the funeral of Tia Nicole Seng. Beautiful Tia. Kind, smart, gentle twenty-two-year-old Tia.

Who no longer exists.

The Seng family files in and sits in the front pew. Tia's parents, small and dignified. Leo and Dr. Vic holding up their grandmother.

My head throbs under the bandage on my forehead. Hurts like hell. And I'm grateful for it, because it means I can still feel something.

Summer stands alone. Her golden hair pulled back, her black suit understated rich-girl perfection. I picture her naked body, remember her crying out for me. It's the only time she isn't utterly self-contained.

Rick sits in his wheelchair, both of Becky's arms around his neck. He holds her hands. He looks more frail than ever, but he insisted on coming. Shane didn't. I offered to help him get here, but he fixed those angry eyes on me and said when you're dead, you're dead, man.

No point.

Chad and Zoey have their arms around each other, holding each other up, maybe. She chose him, not me, for support, physical contact. Her face is pale, eyes red. She looks like hell, and I love her for being so human.

Have you ever *been in love?*

I have insomnia. So sometimes I walk in the dunes. . . .

Oh, Zoey. You and I are not destined for hot sex in the moonlight. I was right about you from the start. You're a love-and-marriage kinda woman. And I am not a love-and-marriage kinda guy. I don't even know what love *is.*

Not that kind of love, anyway.

Now Zoey's crying and Chad is stroking her hair. I want to pull him off her and wrap my arms around her.

Schlitz.

The service begins with a prayer. Then the minister talks about Tia's family. Says that Tia's grandmother and parents escaped the terror of the Khmer Rouge in Cambodia. How much they all love America. How proud they are of their children. Of Tia, their angel.

A Seng cousin—a little girl with a heavenly

voice—sings a hymn. Then Leo speaks. And Dr. Vic.

Tears flow. Outside, the gray sky opens up, and the God or gods above, whatever that means, begin to cry, too.

We're all at the Sengs' house, crowded into their small living room, making post-funeral small talk. This sucks. I'd be praying better if I were on Sunset Beach on Oahu riding a real wave.

If Stevie doesn't make it, will I be crowding into his mom's trailer after some bogus funeral?

No. Uh-uh. That can't happen. Can. Not. Happen.

I've had enough death for a while, thank you.

The Virus is in the dining room talking with Tia's parents. She looks almost human. She acted almost human when she came to see me in the hospital yesterday, too. Seemed actually to care about my well-being. Didn't blame the freak accident on us, either, though I figured for sure she'd see it as a chance to deep-six the Grateful Reds.

She takes Mrs. Seng's hand. Says something. Hugs her. The Virus? Hugging? It thaws out her frigid beauty, like the first jonquil of spring. Weird.

Everyone from FHUH is here, it looks like. That son of a bitch Davis. Agonetti. Bailey with a middle-aged, bone-thin woman in a designer suit. Must be his wife. She has beautiful, graceful hands. I'm insane to notice things like that. Especially at a time like this.

But I do.

Macho man Marcus talks with Hirsute and her significant other. He looks shattered. Michelle, Lark, other nurses cry all over each other.

Lark Peyton, Stevie's red-haired fantasy princess, spies me. Bottom lip quivering, she throws herself into my arms, cries on my shoulder. I reach to give her my red bandanna, then remember. Zoey still has it.

"Tia was the best nurse in the whole hospital," Lark says, sobbing. "The nicest, too."

I agree.

Lark tries to smile. "I know she's gone on to a better place. God must need her even more than we do, huh?"

Those cliché-ridden platitudes make me sick. I OD'd on them years ago. But if they work for Lark, hey, whatever gets you through the night. Or day. Or both.

So I go for the noncommittal half-smile.

Someone knocks on the open front door behind me.

A TV news crew, peering inside, looking for the human-interest story.

I go to the door. "The Seng family wishes me to tell you to go to hell," I say pleasantly. Then I step outside to make sure they actually leave.

The rain has stopped, finally, but it's chilly and windy. Still, I can't bear to go back into that suffocating crush. So I take a walk around the house, into the perfect pruned suburban backyard.

And there's Zee.

Alone.

Her head tilts up to the slate sky. I walk over to her. She doesn't move. But I know she knows I'm there.

"I had this Sunday school teacher when I was a kid," she says, "who told us to write what God looks like. Most of the kids said he looked like a king, sitting up there on a throne in the clouds. Something like that. But I said maybe he *was* the clouds."

"Deep kid," I say.

"My parents never bought that old-guy-on-a-throne thing." She shrugs, wraps her arms around herself. "They really weren't into organized religion, but in Chaney, church was where you went because all your neighbors went."

"Chaney?"

"Oklahoma. Home. After my parents died, my brother sold the place. That was four years ago. I haven't been back since." She finally looks at me. "Funerals suck."

Her brown eyes are luminous. I smell the sweetness of her hair. Singularly Zoey. My hand goes to touch it. Her eyes close. I can't help it. I pull her into my arms. The feel of her is everything. The fit perfect.

Then she's crying. I am the world's biggest schmuck. I pay attention to the sweetness of her hair, the feel of her, and what she wants is comfort from me. Nothing more.

Giving her more would be a lie, anyway. Just my messed-up way of comforting myself.

So we stand there. Like that. The rain starts anew, but we move not at all.

15
ZOEY

Walking in the rain. Sounds romantic. But really it's just wet. And cold. I and my mind walked for hours in the rain. Life and death. Medicine and me. Chaney and Belle Woods. My mom and my dad. Tia and the kid in the chopper.

The funeral and Tristan.

Mostly Tristan.

If I knew someone as shallow as me, I'd puke.

The truth: Tristan held me in the Sengs' backyard to be nice.

More truth: All I could think about was kissing him. Jumping him. Hot sex, passion, love with him.

I suck.

Had to escape. I did. Rain-soaked beach walk. My reward: wrecked dress shoes. Blisters. Frigid body temp. Read: invitation for a summer cold.

No one home at the unsweet suite. I jump into hot shower and try to scrub off lust for Tristan. Turns out it's a stain. Indelible.

There's a note taped to the coffeemaker.

> Zoey
> Chad and I are meeting Rick and Shane in the secret room Tia found for us. Seems fitting, huh? We can hold a more personal memorial. Fifth floor, old wing, third room on the right. Come be with us.
> Becky

Alone feels too lonely. So I pull on jeans and a sweatshirt, head back to Effing-Huh. Hit the fifth floor. Hit the wing under renovation, but no one's working on Sunday. Looks deserted. Third door on the—? Did Becky say right or left? Third door from elevator or stairs? Third door or third room? What about closets?

Schlitz.

I try doors. Locked. Locked. Locked again. It's a game show. My friends are behind some door. If I find them, Bob'll tell me what I've won.

Try another. Assume it'll be locked like the others. It swings open. It's empty.

Try another. Locked. Another. Open.

Not empty. People.

Summer. Dr. Bailey. She's in his arms.

My mouth flaps like a caught fish's gills. Useless.

I pull the door shut. Heart pounding. Did that really happen?

I expect them to burst into hallway. Make a citizen's arrest. They don't. Maybe neither saw me? Maybe I imagined the whole thing.

Try more doors. The third strikes gold. Chad and Becky and Rick and Shane.

And Tristan.

Uh, Tristan? Your girlfriend is three doors down about to do Dr. Bailey.

My best comebacks are internal. Read: Zoey the wuss steps to the plate again. I don't say it. Don't say anything.

They're buzzed. Feeling merry. Someone got some wine. They're swilling it from Dixie cups. Toasting Tia with sweet-funny moments remembered.

From Chad: Tia scooping vodka from the punch at Leo's party. Too bad she couldn't scoop out LSD.

From Becky: Tia macking with Marcus in supply closet. They backed into a shelf that fell on them.

From Shane: Tia yelling at Leo to get his act together. Then yelling at anyone else who yelled at him.

From Tristan: Tia welcoming the Red Tide. Us. More than anyone else in all of FHUH.

From me: Tia singing with the wigged wonder, Zelda.

Effing-Huh. Tia. Gone.

My Dixie cup is filled. I *never* drink, but I drink to Tia.

Tristan's eyes meet mine. I feel him everywhere.

"This is why you gotta do what you want to do when you want to do it," Chad says, slurring a little.

Bar owner's son, clearly not used to drinking. " 'Cuz you never know, man."

"Tell that to yourself," Tristan advises.

Chad nods. "You're right. I'm giving Eve that letter tomorrow. 'Cuz I love her, man."

Eve? Letter? Cluelessness strikes, but it doesn't matter.

"And I love *her*, man," Rick teases. It's clear he means Becky. Who shares the bed with him. In his arms.

Shane swallows some wine. "Get it while you can, bro, 'cuz you could be chomping worms this time next week."

Becky shoots a dagger look. "So could you."

Shane smiles. "Unlike my blissed-out bro, I'm looking forward to it."

"You don't mean that," Rick insists.

Shane shrugs. "Depends on which day you ask me. Today, I do."

The room goes cold.

"Well, call me crazy, but I'm kinda set on having you hang around," Rick finally says.

Shane scratches his cheek. "Yeah, but you're a butthole."

"You look like a butthole, and you act like one, too!" the twin bros sing together, then crack up. I'm guessing leftover twin childhood-thing.

"Hey, what's that song Tia used to sing with Zelda?" Becky asks. "Some oldie thing."

" 'Bye-bye, Miss American Pie,' " Chad starts singing.

Funny. I feel so much. Like I've known them forever. Like family I lost. And found again.

Funny, too. We all know words to the chorus. We
sing badly. About driving the Chevy to the levee. And
people drinking whiskey and rye. And how this'll be
the day that I die.

An alarm sounds.

First thought: Schlitz. Summer turned us in.

Second thought: Fire alarm. No, no, no.

No time for third thought before truth dawns.

Rick's beeper. Shane's beeper. High-pitched beeping.

Other than that, silence so thick you'd have to cut
it to hear it.

Their beepers *never* beep. Because they only beep
for one reason.

Heart-lung donor match.

But only for one of them.

To be decided on a coin toss.

One brother has a chance. The other will die.

Rick and Shane click off their beepers. Their eyes
lock. Becky's shaking. It barely registers that Tristan
has taken my hand.

Shane's prepared. He reaches into his pocket.

And pulls out a silver dollar.

"Heads or tails, bro'?" he asks Rick. "Call it in
the air."

The silver dollar sails skyward, turning end over
end.

THE END

CHERIE BENNETT and JEFF GOTTESFELD

Cherie Bennett and her husband, Jeff Gottesfeld, often write on teen themes. This novel is their latest for Berkley; they wrote the *Trash* series together, while Cherie authored the best-selling Berkley series *Sunset Island*. Cherie writes both paperback and hardcover fiction—*Life in the Fat Lane*, *Zink*—while her Copley News Service syndicated column, "Hey Cherie!" appears in papers coast to coast. She is also one of America's finest young playwrights and a back-to-back winner of The Kennedy Center's "New Visions/ New Voices" playwriting award. Cherie and Jeff live in Nashville and Los Angeles, and may always be contacted at P.O. Box 150326, Nashville, TN 37215; e-mail to authorchik@aol.com